Affair *of the* Heart

Follow Your Heart!

Carol
Maguire

SKYE SERIES

Affair of the Heart

by
CAROL DUERKSEN & MAYNARD KNEPP

WILLOWSPRING DOWNS

Affair of the Heart
Book 2 — Skye Series
Copyright © 1998 by WillowSpring Downs

First Printing, 1998

Printed in the United States of America

Cover illustration by Susan Bartel

Page design & layout by Good Shepherd Publications, Hillsboro, Kansas. Web site: www.gspbooks.com

All rights reserved. No part of this publication may be reproduced in any form or by any means without the prior written permission of the publisher. For information, write to WillowSpring Downs, Route 2, Box 31, Hillsboro, KS 67063.

This story is a fictional account of an Amish and Mennonite family. Names, characters, places and incidents are either imaginary or are used fictitiously, and their resemblance, if any, to real persons, living or dead, is purely coincidental.

Library of Congress Catalog Number 98-61365
ISBN 0-9648525-8-6

Acknowledgments

The following friends and family members were invaluable in making *Affair of the Heart* a reality. They supported and encouraged us, critiqued the manuscript, and shared their time and expertise. Thank you so much to:

Charity Bucher	Leanne Githens
Talon Bunn	Eddy Hall
Tom and Connie Bunn	Sonja Hoffmann
Gary Duerksen	Cindy Hastings
Marlo Duerksen	Judy Jordan
Milton and Alice Duerksen	Laurie L. Oswald
Mary Lou Farmer	Mary Ulsaker

And Molly Lou the cat, who sat on my lap and purred her encouragement as I wrote.

Bo

BO

ONE

Bo RIGGS leaned against the tall Kansas cottonwood tree and smiled. It was one of those smiles that starts deep down in the heart and spreads through every tissue of a man's body. It was one of those smiles that, by the time it gets to the face, has saturated a guy's soul with happiness. It was a smile of excitement, contentment and, above all, amazement. He still couldn't quite believe this was happening to him.

But the proof hummed in the activity around him. At 8:00 a.m. on this morning of June 2, the Amish farmstead nearly sang with anticipation. From the concentric semicircles of wooden plank seats under trees across the yard from him to the shiny Harley-Davidson motorcycle beside his leg, the preparations were nearly done. He had no doubt that Becca, Emma and all of Skye's other female relatives had the food well on its way. It'd be a feast for sure, Amish style.

"Hey, Bo, can you give me a ride?" The young boy's voice came closer with each word, and Bo turned to see Matt Swartzendruber running toward him as fast as his six-year-old legs could bring him. "Please, Bo, please?" he begged breathlessly. "Can you?"

Bo laughed, a deep low laugh that rumbled in his throat. "Matt, Matt, you can't get enough, can you?"

"I'm going to have a Harley just like you and Aunt Skye," Matt said, trying to climb onto the bike.

"I'm sure you will," Bo agreed, helping Matt straddle the seat. "And will you give me a ride then?"

Matt giggled as if that was the funniest thing he'd ever heard, but he would not be deterred from his mission. "Can we go for a ride?"

Bo glanced at his watch before answering. "I don't know, Matt. There's probably something I should be doing to get ready for the wedding."

"Just a little ride!"

"Okay, run and get your helmet."

Matt scrambled down from the bike and was gone. Bo chuckled. Motorcycle rides on an Amish farmstead. And he knew that was only the beginning of a day full of paradoxes.

"A short ride," Bo had promised Matt as they left the farmyard and turned right down the sand road. Bo could see black buggies in the distance, coming toward them. People were coming to his wedding, and he was leaving the yard. They'd be talking about that for sure, he grinned. Oh well, it wouldn't be the first, or the last, time this community would have something to say about its newest members.

He hadn't been sure what to think when Skye suggested they buy a small plot of land from her grandfather and build a house on it. For one thing, it would mean an hour's drive to his shop in Vicksburg. He figured he could handle that, but the idea of living in a small community where everybody knew everybody else's business. . .well that would take some getting used to. He was, after all, a Harley man. His business was Harleys and, yes, some leather. He looked and dressed the part. Even today.

Bo grinned wide and nodded at the first buggy as it approached them. Inside, a young man in a black-brimmed hat waved, while his wife and a sea of children's faces only stared. Bo laughed.

"Whatcha laughing at?" Matt asked from behind Bo, his arms wrapped tightly around Bo's waist.

"Oh, nothing," Bo answered.

"Can I have a ride in one of those?" Bo could feel that Matt had twisted around to watch the buggy go by.

"Didn't look like there was much room in that one," Bo chuckled. "But I'm sure we can get somebody in your Aunt Skye's family to give you a ride later today. Okay?"

"Okay," Matt agreed. "Now can we go fast on the cycle?"

"Nope," Bo answered, noticing a growing line of buggies moving toward the farm. Unless he wanted to meet each one of them, he should turn around and go back. Skye was probably fit to be tied, wondering what happened to him. For all her independence, she seemed to want to keep a close eye on him. He didn't mind, really. Skye was Skye.

Skye. As he slowly turned the Harley around and rumbled back to the farmstead, he remembered the first time he met her, and saw this Amish home. It had all been the same day, exactly a year ago.

A big diesel bus had pulled into the parking lot of his Harley-Davidson store in Vicksburg. He'd recognized Skye the minute she stepped from the bus, followed by her band members. She was one of the hottest up-and-coming rock artists, and something had clicked between them that morning in the shop. Chemistry. At first, he'd thought it was just him. Then, he felt it coming from her. But that's the way she is with a lot of men, he'd told himself. Be cool. She's here to look at bikes, not to pick up a date.

As it happened, she got both, he smiled to himself as he turned into the driveway. Because the next thing he knew, Skye was pouting about not being able to drive a Harley out to see her Amish grandparents, and he was offering to take her. Less than two hours after meeting her, he was meeting part of her family in this very yard. As her chauffeur, of course. Who would have predicted. . . .

"Hey, Luke, look at me! I'm getting a ride," Matt was yelling at his brother as they rolled slowly down the lane.

Yes, who would have predicted he'd be marrying Skye a year later, and giving rides to the sons her sister Angela left behind. . . .

"I want one too!" Luke was running toward them. Two years older than Matt, he obviously couldn't stand his brother getting something he didn't. "Bo! It's my turn!"

"Later, Luke, later," Bo said, helping Matt off of the bike. "I've got a wedding to go to now."

Bo could feel the eyes of the wedding guests on him as he walked his bike back to the big tree he'd been standing under earlier. Some people were starting to fill in the seats, others stood around talking. Buggies and cars continued to roll slowly onto the yard, past the two houses, barns and outbuildings, and to the field that had been designated for parking. He'd known it would be this way, but he couldn't help grinning with delight at the assortment of people at the wedding. On Skye's side of the family, there were the conservatively dressed Amish people who had arrived in their horse-and-buggy rigs, as well as her Mennonite relatives from Pennsylvania. Skye's parents, Ken and Becca, were there of course, along with Ken's two brothers. Skye's brother-in-law, Jon Swartzendruber, had driven from Iowa with his three young sons. There was only one thing that could make this day better, Bo thought, and that was if Angela were still alive. He couldn't imagine how much Jon and the boys must miss their wife and mother. He knew her death still haunted Skye at times, and she'd cried more than once during their wedding preparations, wishing her twin sister could be there.

Bo didn't know what it would be like to have a brother or sister—he was an only child. He looked around for his parents and saw them standing near the house, visiting with Skye's grandfather Jonas. Leave it to the friendly old Amish minister to make his parents feel at home.

And then there were the bikers—Bo's friends who'd rumbled onto the yard on their Harleys. Like the Amish men, they were dressed in black too, but their black was leather. Leather accented with chains. Bo's grin split his face at the incongruity of it all. What a marriage this was going to be!

He strode through the gathering people toward the house and went inside. The bright open Amish home smelled of food preparations, and suddenly he could hardly wait to eat. He realized he'd been up a long time and hadn't stopped for breakfast. One more hour, and he'd be digging into the feast with his new bride beside him.

"Are you ready, Bo?" the question came from Skye's mother Becca, who'd just emerged from one of the bedrooms.

"Ready as I'll ever be," Bo's low voice responded. "Question is, are you ready to have me in your family?"

"You know we are," Becca said, putting one arm around Bo and looking up at him. "If somebody would have told me when I was a little Amish girl that someday my daughter would be marrying the likes of you, I'd have said they were crazy," Becca laughed. "But life has a way of throwing unexpected things at us, doesn't it?" She grew serious as she continued. "Like the twins. God gave us Skye and Angela in such a strange way. But what a blessing they were. And then, Angela gave up her kidney, and her life, for Skye." Becca turned away from Bo, and he saw her eyes glisten.

"I'm sure Angela's watching today," he said softly.

"I know," Becca agreed, wiping at her eyes. "It's still hard, sometimes."

The bedroom door opened and Skye walked out. Bo looked up, and the excited, yet contented, amazement he'd felt earlier seized him again. Skye was 35 and a rock star. She'd been places and done things a person wouldn't talk about too loudly among her Amish relatives. But during the last year, since her sister's death, Skye had changed. She'd stopped her road tours, and had concentrated on recording in a studio. She'd taken care of herself, watched her diet, managed her diabetes. She'd replaced her alcohol addiction with one of walking. She'd told him yesterday she'd never felt better. He doubted she'd ever looked better.

Yes, she was looking good. Skye's blonde hair was tied up in sunflowers at the back of her head, and her green eyes sparkled. She probably didn't weigh a pound more than she had at 20, he surmised, his eyes traveling down Skye's body. They'd talked a long time about what to wear for their wedding, finally settling on black jeans, white shirt and black leather vest for him, and a wonderful white dress for Skye. Not the traditional bridal dress, by any means. That wouldn't be Skye. This dress was a creation from Skye's mind and a seamstress she had hired, and Bo loved the results—a neckline high enough to be modest and low enough to make him smile, a bodice that highlighted Skye's small waist, and a full skirt that would swing wonderfully at the dance later that evening.

"You look great," Bo said, reaching for Skye's hands and losing himself in her eyes.

"I'm a very lucky woman today," she answered, placing his hands on her waist and reaching up with her fingers to his face. She kissed him lightly and said, "That was a beginning. More later."

"I can hardly wait," he said quietly, in the voice he knew Skye loved. "But in the meantime, we have a wedding to go to."

He took her hand and they walked toward the door. The kitchen clock said 8:55.

BO

TWO

Bo AND SKYE stepped out of the house and into their wedding sanctuary. The farmstead belonged to Jonas and Sue Ann Bontrager, and to their youngest daughter, Emma, and her husband, Caleb. Their houses flanked either side of a lane lined with cottonwood trees. On Jonas and Sue Ann's side of the lane, a grove of larger cottonwoods formed a backdrop for their house, and it was toward this grove that Bo and Skye proceeded. Seated on the wooden planks, the guests were listening to a small orchestra in the center of the semicircle. Music had always been a part of Skye's life, and the orchestra had been her idea.

While the couple waited near the house, the orchestra finished the prelude. Then, after a momentary pause, the strains of Pachelbel's beautiful Canon in D began sifting over the audience, through sun-kissed leaves in the trees, over immaculate flower beds, toward Bo and Skye. Bo closed his eyes and welcomed the music into his soul. He'd never heard the Canon in D until Skye introduced him to it, and he'd never in his life been so moved by a piece of music. Now, with the vibrant warmth of Skye beside him and the sun shining through his closed eyelids, he knew a tough, 40-year-old Harley man could cry. He could cry for the absolute joy of it all.

Bo followed the music with his heart, and when he finally

opened his eyes, he saw that the mist in his was matched by the shining in Skye's. He squeezed her hand, and they began walking to the semicircle. Reaching it, they continued until they were standing next to the orchestra. The music swelled and celebrated the moment, and Bo turned to Skye. Their eyes locked, and remained that way until the last note of the violin faded away.

Skye smiled at him, and then she turned toward the guests. "We'd like to welcome you to our wedding," she said. "Our God, who is more loving and powerful than any of us will ever understand, has brought us all here together today, and for that Bo and I are so grateful."

Bo nodded in agreement. There was still a lot of this God-stuff he had to get used to. Neither he nor Skye had had much to do with God when they first met. But Angela's death had changed all that. The total unexpectedness of it had shocked him into realizing that there were no guarantees in life, and that he'd better evaluate his relationship with God. But it was Angela's note that brought both him and Skye to their knees. Angela's husband, Jon, had found the note to her family in her dresser. She said she was having a strange feeling about the surgery, and just wanted them to know how much she loved them. And if anything went wrong, she wanted them to know she wouldn't change a thing "for all the stars in the sky." That phrase was from a song Skye wrote when they were in high school—a song Skye continued to sing at every concert she did when she was on the road. The song ended with the words "And the good Lord will remain to lead the way." And that's how Angela had ended her note: "Remember that I love you, and that no matter what happens in your life, the good Lord will remain to lead the way."

Angela hadn't lived through the kidney transplant, but her healthy kidney saved Skye's life. And in the process of giving Skye her physical life, she had also opened Skye's and Bo's souls to a new spiritual life as well. The good Lord certainly had remained to lead the way, Bo thought.

But there was still so much he didn't know. Like the hymn everyone was singing right now. "Everybody knows 'The Love of God,'" Skye had said when they were planning the wedding. Well, he and his Harley buddies weren't everybody. They hadn't grown up in the church like Skye. She knew the hymns, she knew the Bible—she'd known it with her head for years. Now her heart was into it too. For Bo, well, his heart was with God, but he felt like he was on a bike trip and he didn't know what he was going to run into along the way. He glanced at the section where his friends were sitting. Some were studying the hymnbooks, trying to follow along. Rowdy, his best friend, grinned and gestured with his palms up in the air in a "I give up" motion, and another one gave Bo the thumbs up. Bo wanted to motion back, but thought better of it.

The hymn over, the pastor of the Wellsford Mennonite Church stood up. Bo and Skye had been attending the church for a few months, and although Bo still felt like an outsider, Marge Enninger had quickly made them feel welcome and befriended them. Bo liked her, and it seemed logical to involve her in their wedding.

"Skye and Bo have chosen several passages for their marriage service this morning," Pastor Marge said. "First, from the Song of Solomon, chapter 2, verses 10-13. 'My beloved speaks and says to me: Arise, my love, my fair one, and come away; for now the winter is past, the rain is over and gone. The flowers appear on the earth; the time of singing has come, and the voice of the turtledove is heard in our land. The fig tree puts forth its figs, and the vines are in blossom; they give forth fragrance. Arise, my love, my fair one, and come away.'"

Pastor Marge sat back down, and Bo's heart skipped several beats. As far as Skye knew, the next part of the service was a musical piece by the orchestra. But Bo had made other arrangements. Against his better judgment, he was going to sing a song to Skye. A song that he'd written. He knew he couldn't compete with Skye's voice or her song-writing abilities, but he'd played around with his guitar for years. Just for fun. One evening, shortly after they'd decided to get married, the song had showed up in his mind and through his fingers. He'd known then it was a gift he wanted to share with Skye. Oh, the pain of hiding it from her! He should be glad the wait was over, and he could sing the song. But he was scared. Maybe he could still back out.

No. Young Luke was already walking up to Bo, right on cue, carrying Bo's guitar. Behind him was Luke's father, Jon, carrying two bar stools.

"Skye, you don't know about this," Bo's voice trembled and his hands shook as he took the guitar from Luke. "But I'd like to sing you a song right now. Please, have a chair."

The surprised look on Skye's face matched what Bo had anticipated, but he was too nervous to really enjoy the moment. Skye slipped up onto one of the stools, and Bo onto the other one. He began picking the tune, and the words followed.

I will take your hand,
If you will hold mine too.
And I will be your man
Only if you want me to.
I can't give you everything
you'll ever want and more,
But I will hold you in my arms
like never before.

And I'll take you to the same place
we first kissed and fell in love.
And I'll sing you our favorite song
'til you can't get enough.
And we'll slow dance until the

last stars fade into dawn.
Darling, it was you all along.

Don't always come easy
Like it has for us,
And with this ring I'm promising
Never to let up.
Girl, you were my first love
And you'll be the last I know,
And I will follow you right down
Any road you go.

And I'll take you to the same place
We first kissed and fell in love.
And I'll sing you our favorite song
'Til you can't get enough.
And we'll slow dance until the
last stars fade into dawn.
Darling, it was you all along.
Darling, it's been you all along.*

    The last word. The last chord. It wasn't until then that Bo dared look up from his guitar to the woman seated beside him. He'd been afraid he couldn't get through the song if he'd looked at Skye, and now he knew he was right. Tears flooded her bright eyes and spilled down her cheeks. She stood up and came to him, and for a moment, no one else existed.
    Then the applause began, bringing them back. His arm around Skye, Bo nodded at the guests and mumbled, "Thank you." Soon the clapping was joined by whistles from the Harley section, and Bo found himself blushing. *Okay, enough already,* he thought.

---

* *"All Along,"* © *1997 by Jake Schmidt*

Pastor Marge stepped in at that point, and the applause faded away. She looked at Bo, then at Skye. "All I can say is, I can't wait to get you two in our choir."

Everyone laughed lightly, and then Pastor Marge continued. "We're going to have a time of sharing now. What words of encouragement and advice do you bring to Skye and Bo this morning? What would you want them to know, from your experience? What do you feel God would want them to hear on this, their wedding day?"

Bo and Skye had asked several people to be prepared for this time in the service, but they were also hoping that others would talk. Skye's parents were the first to stand up and come to the front. Becca was carrying a large, flat object under her arm.

Bo smiled at Ken and Becca. He was just getting to know them, since they lived in Pennsylvania. He'd been apprehensive when he'd heard that Skye's parents were Mennonites. What would Mennonites think of their daughter marrying the owner of a Harley-Davidson store? Would they assume he was a rough and tough, booze-guzzling, living-on-the-edge kind of guy? Would they hold that stereotype against him even if it wasn't true, at least not anymore?

Yes, he had felt their unspoken questions when they first met. And he'd done everything he could to show them that his heart, beneath the black leather, was in the right place. He only wanted to marry their daughter and be the best husband he could be. He hoped with all his being that they trusted him and his intentions.

"Skye and Bo," the words were coming from Ken, and Bo could sense his nervousness. "Becca and I talked a long time about what we would say to you this morning." Ken paused, licked his lips, glanced at Becca, then continued. "We finally decided to bring you a picture, and to talk about it briefly."

Becca held up the object she'd been carrying, and Bo heard

Skye whisper beside him, "Oh my goodness."

He'd seen the picture before, but he didn't know when or where. It was a painting of Jesus, holding a lamb.

"Skye will recognize this picture as the one we've had in our bedroom since the day we were married. It was a wedding present from my grandmother," Ken continued. "Skye will also remember hearing a story about how this picture played an important role in her birth," Ken paused again, and Bo could feel the anticipation among the wedding guests and within himself. What did this picture have to do with Skye's birth?

"As some, but not all, of you know, Skye and her twin sister were born at our house 35 years ago to a teenage girl named Andrea," Ken continued. "Andrea used this picture to focus on during the labor, and she told the girls in a letter that she had to believe that if Jesus cared for little lost lambs, surely he would care for her little girls."

Ken stopped and looked at Becca, who continued, "And God has taken care of you, Skye. You've been through a lot." Becca stopped, and Bo knew this was hard for her to do. "We want you to have this picture as you and Bo begin your married life together. We hope it will symbolize Jesus' love for you—a love that never gives up on any of us."

Becca stepped toward Skye and Bo to hand them the painting, and they embraced her and Ken. The Harley man's heart knew he'd never been through anything like this before, and the service wasn't over yet.

BO

THREE

THE PERSONAL, heartfelt sharing during Skye and Bo's wedding service continued with Skye's grandmother on her father Ken's side. Leanne was in her late 70's—a short, plump woman who wore the white prayer covering of her conservative group of Mennonites. Leanne had lost her husband in an accident when Ken was in college. She spoke of what it means to have a good marriage and the importance of making every day count. She ended it by repeating a quote that had meant a lot to Ken's father. "It's from Winston Churchill," she said, "and it says this: 'We make a living by what we get, but we make a life by what we give.' Skye and Bo, it is my prayer that you will take that philosophy to heart in your life together. May God bless you."

As Leanne was walking back to her seat, Luke and Matt Swartzendruber came toward the front, followed by their father, Jon, who was carrying three-year-old Mark. Luke and Matt came to stand next to Bo and looked up at him, and he grinned back down at them. They'd been hit with a severe case of Uncle Bo-admiration, he could see, and it tickled him.

"Skye and Bo, we're here just to say that we're happy for you today," Jon began. "As you know, my boys are thrilled to have an uncle who'll give them cycle rides, and I'm guessing in a few years they'll be in that shop of yours begging you for something else—

only then it'll be a special deal on a Harley they'll be wanting." Jon paused as the guests laughed lightly, and then he continued. "Seeing you today, Skye, reminds me so much of Angela." Jon stopped, and Bo watched the struggle emerge on his face. The tall, strong Iowa farmer had been determined to get through this without breaking down, Bo knew, but a powerful surge of emotion had swept through Jon and was threatening to destroy his determination. "Angela was everything a guy could want in a wife and mother for his children," Jon continued. "You. . .you were twins. You have all of those wonderful traits in you too, Skye. I. . .I wish the best for you as you share yourself with Bo. Bo, you're a lucky guy."

Bo felt the tears in his eyes that he saw in Jon's. He wanted to acknowledge Jon's pain somehow, but Skye was already there, her arms wrapped around Jon and Mark. Bo waited until Skye stepped back, then took his turn to embrace Jon. On the day that he was gaining a wife, this man was grieving the loss of his. There was no way to ease that hurt except to stand beside him.

Jon turned to walk back, his boys behind him, and Bo reached for the handkerchief he'd put in his jeans pocket at the last minute.

* * *

Bo and Skye knew there were risks involved in asking people to share at their wedding. There were no guarantees that someone wouldn't say or do something embarrassing—either to them or to the other guests. Someone like Rowdy, for example.

Bo got worried the minute he saw his Harley friend Rowdy stand up and swagger his way toward them. Don't do it, Rowdy, Bo pleaded silently. Don't make us all look bad in front of these Amish people. Please don't do it.

Rowdy was wearing his best black Harley T-shirt, black jeans and black boots. His concession to the occasion, it appeared to

Bo, was that he'd exchanged the large hoop earrings he usually wore in his left ear for small gold studs. He'd been balding for years, and the little hair that did come in he shaved as quickly as it showed up. His shaver, however, never made it down as far as his chin, and Rowdy sported a heavy brown beard that looked a whole lot like the ones on the Amish men at the wedding.

"I've been thinkin' long and hard 'bout what to say to ya'll," Rowdy had stationed himself between Bo and Skye and placed a grease-stained hand on each of their shoulders. "I finally decided maybe I should tell a joke."

Bo turned his head sharply toward Rowdy and pleaded with his eyes. No, Rowdy, no. Don't do it!

"Seems like there was this Amish couple who just got married," Rowdy began, and Bo groaned inwardly. He was about to do bodily harm to that friend of his. "They went to a motel for their wedding night, and when they checked in, well, the gal at the desk took one look at them and asked, 'You're newlyweds, aren't you?' The Amish guy kinda blushed and said 'Yah.' The gal smiled at them both and said 'In that case, I'm sure you'll be wanting the bridal suite.'

"The Amish guy looked a little puzzled, but then he smiled real big and said, 'Oh no, I won't be needing a bridle, I'll just'"— Bo's hand clapped firmly around Rowdy's mouth, and a wave of laughter rippled through the guests. "You don't need a bridle, you need a muzzle!" Bo threatened his friend, and the laughter exploded.

"It's a great joke," Rowdy grinned at the guests, his hands in his pockets. "Look me up later and I'll finish it for you."

"*I'll* look you up later, and I'll finish *you*," Bo promised. "Now please go back to your seat and be quiet."

Rowdy hung his head down like a naughty little boy and swaggered back, much to the amusement of the audience.

Bo glanced at Skye, wondering how she'd taken Rowdy's

behavior. He was relieved to see that "Whatever" look on her face, and he relaxed. He turned toward the guests again, and saw Skye's grandfather Jonas slowly making his way toward them.

Being in his early 80's had slowed Jonas Bontrager's body down a bit, but not his mind. He still preached, unrehearsed and without notes, at every Amish church service. He was well respected among the Amish in many communities because he was fair, had a great sense of humor, and could get along with almost anyone. Now, dressed in his black Sunday jacket and homemade pants, with his long flowing beard and silky white hair shining in the sun, he commanded instant respect from the audience. Some of them, especially Bo's friends, had never been that close to an Amish minister.

"I don't know if that joke was my cue to come up here or not," Jonas said, gazing across the guests with his bright blue eyes. "I am Amish, but I don't know the punch line either." A wave of relief and appreciation for the elderly man filled Bo.

"I must say, I've never been to a wedding like this," Jonas continued. "But I have never met people quite like Skye and Bo either, so I guess this shouldn't surprise me," he looked at the couple, and they smiled back at him. "I have known Skye since she was a baby, but I always regretted that her parents didn't live closer so her grandmother and I would have had more time with her and Angela," he paused briefly before continuing. "The time they spent with us here on the farm during the summer was always a highlight for us.

"I remember one summer when Skye and Angela were about seven years old. That was the summer Angela learned to play the hamonica, but Skye just didn't quite have the patience to practice like her sister did." Bo glanced at Skye. A mixture of memories was reflected in her green eyes as she listened to her grandfather.

"I won't tell the whole story—you can get that from Skye if you want to, and be sure to ask her about the outhouse." Jonas's wrinkled face grinned at Skye, then he continued, "But I will say that there were some tears in the process. I gave her one of my bandannas when she was crying, and told her she could keep it for other times in her life when she needed to cry. I hear she still has that bandanna, and that it's been places no other Amish bandanna would dare go."

The guests laughed, and Bo could hear Skye giggling beside him. Jonas was right about that—her bandanna had been with her at every single concert she ever gave. A sort of good-luck charm, she'd told Bo.

"Now Skye is getting married, and she and Bo will be living here near us. I guess they probably won't be farmers, but if they live on my land, I think they should each have a new bandanna."

Jonas reached into the side pockets of his barn-door pants, and from each pocket he pulled a neatly folded red handkerchief. He handed one to Bo, and one to Skye.

"Oh, and there's one more thing," Jonas added. "Skye, there's something in yours. Maybe now that you're older you'll want to try it again."

Bo watched as Skye unfolded her bandanna. A silver harmonica glinted in the sunshine.

₰ ₰ ₰

The wedding vows Bo and Skye had written for their marriage ceremony symbolized who they were, what they were bringing to the marriage, and how they viewed their commitment to each other. They had decided to say the vows to each other, without the assistance of Pastor Marge. "Unless we get totally stuck," Bo had said at the rehearsal. "Then please step in and rescue us!"

Following a brief meditation by Pastor Marge, Bo and Skye stood hand in hand, facing their guests. Bo was nervous again. He didn't want to forget the words—that would be so embarrassing. He'd thought about writing them on a card that he could read, but then told himself he surely should be able to memorize something as important as his wedding vows. So he had. Now if he could just get through them as easily as he had this morning when he was practicing.

"We believe in a great and awesome God who created the universe and who created us," Bo and Skye said together. "We believe in God's son, Jesus, the Lord of our lives. We believe in the Holy Spirit, the one who fills and enriches our lives. We believe that God has brought us together to share the rest of our lives with each other."

At that point, Bo and Skye turned toward each other, and Bo listened as Skye recited:

"Today, in the presence of our families, friends, and God, I commit myself to you. I will be with you to share the bad times as well as the good times. I will give you the space you need to be yourself and to grow as an individual, and I will also walk very close to you and be your best friend, your helper, your lover, your playmate. I love you, Bo, and I am looking forward to spending my life with you."

Now it was his turn. He knew the words. He'd known as he heard Skye say them that they were becoming ingrained not just in his mind but in his heart. He knew the words, and he could hardly wait to say them, and he could hardly wait to live them.

And so they flowed out of him without a falter. And when he was done, Skye's eyes said it all. She was his only one.

They exchanged rings and kissed as a cardinal sang loudly in a nearby cottonwood tree. The orchestra began to play, and the service was over except for the leaving. Ah, yes, the leaving. Bo grinned as he took his smiling wife by the hand and led her to the Harley-Davidson leaning against the tree. She slid on the back of the seat, he slipped in front of her, and he felt her arms wrap tightly around his waist. For a moment he could hear the tittering laughter from the audience, and then it was drowned out in the rumble-purr of the Harley engine beneath him. He donned his sunglasses, looked back at Skye, and then swung the bike around and past the orchestra. He revved the throttle, the bike jumped, and they roared past the guests and down the lane.

Somewhere behind them, the people smiled and shook their heads, the orchestra finished its postlude, and an old Amish minister pondered it all in his heart.

After a quick spin down the road, Bo and Skye returned to the farmyard to invite their guests to stay for the meal and an afternoon of music and socializing. Bo's hunger had disappeared during the service, but now it was back in full force, and he could hardly wait to eat. The kitchen helpers were filling the tables set up outside with steaming bowls of fried chicken, mashed potatoes, gravy, noodles, corn, salads, homemade applesauce, and hot rolls. Bo knew he'd be stuffed after that, and he also knew he'd make a trip to the dessert table to find pies, cakes, and puddings, and he'd have some of that too. And then he'd be miserable. One miserable, happy man.

BO
FOUR

EVERYBODY in the Wellsford community was talking about the wedding. Everybody who had been there was, of course, talking because they'd seen it all, firsthand. And those who hadn't been in attendance were asking questions and repeating what so-and-so had said.

"Did one of those motorcycle guys really tell a bad joke during the wedding?"

"I heard they almost ran over somebody with the cycle on the way out!"

"They say that Bo can really sing good!"

"I thought Skye was the singer!"

"I heard that Skye's parents from Pennsylvania cried when they gave her that picture—why would you give away something that meant that much?"

"Those three little Swartzendruber boys were sure cute—that's so sad they don't have a mother. I don't see how Skye can live with that."

"Did you hear what Jonas Bontrager did? Gave them bandannas and a harmonica!"

"What do you think minister Jonas thought about a woman being up there, being the preacher?"

"I guess the vows included God in them at least, didn't they?

At least somebody told me they did. Makes you wonder though, with some of the other stuff at that wedding."

"Yeah, I was there. Can't say I'd do my wedding that way, but you know, it fit them."

The details of Skye and Bo's wedding floated through the community on wagging tongues. Some were positive, some negative, and some just shook their heads and said it was different. Bo had known it would be that way—he'd also hoped most of it would be over by the time he and Skye got back from their honeymoon bike trip to Arkansas. And it was, for the most part.

The day they got back—a week after the wedding—Bo was in the Wellsford Hardware Store buying a few things. He noticed that an Amish man who was also in the store seemed to be watching him, and when Bo went to the checkout register, the man followed. He looked to be about Bo's age—tall, with a dark brown beard, the customary straw hat, worn denim pants, and light cotton shirt. He leaned on the counter and watched as Bo paid for his supplies, and Bo caught him staring at the shiny gold band on his finger.

"So then, your wife, she didn't grow up with her real parents?" the man said, and Bo looked at him with more than a little surprise on his face.

"Uh, no. No, she didn't," Bo said, searching the bearded face for an explanation.

"Actually, she did," he continued. "Ken and Becca are about as real as anybody I know. But if you mean are they her biological parents, no, they aren't."

"That's what I meant," the Amish man returned Bo's gaze, and then abruptly changed the subject. "So, you likin' it, livin' out there in the country?"

"Don't know yet, since we just got back," Bo replied. "But I think it'll be great. By the way, I don't think I know you. My name's Bo—Bo Riggs."

"Ezra Yoder," the man answered. "Be seein' you around," he said, and strolled out of the store.

Ezra Yoder. Bo had no idea who he was, or why he'd ask about Skye's real parents, as he called them. Could be just curious, Bo thought. Still, it seemed like a strange thing to ask.

Bo forgot about the encounter with Ezra as he rode his cycle from the small town of Wellsford back to his new home five miles out in the country. He passed field upon field of golden wheat, basking in the hot June sun, going through the final ripening stages. Farmers would be in the fields with their combines in about ten days, he figured. If the weather cooperated, June 20 was usually a pretty good estimate on the beginning of harvest.

He'd always viewed wheat harvest as a passerby, knowing it was a stressful, exciting, go-for-it highlight of the year for farmers in the Wellsford community, but not actually being a part of the activity. This year, he could participate if he wanted to—Emma's husband, Caleb, had said he could use an extra hand if Bo wanted to help after he got home from work at the store. Bo figured it'd be a great way to get to know Skye's family and some other members of the community.

Bo came up behind a team of horses pulling a manure spreader, and the pungent aroma saturated his senses. Living in the country was one thing, he mused. Living near Amish farmers who used natural fertilizer on their fields was an aspect he'd have to get used to. He pulled out around the team and waved at the boy standing on the spreader. The kid can't be more than eight, Bo thought, and he's handling four Belgians that probably weigh more than 1,500 pounds each. Amazing.

Bo passed several more farmers with their horse-drawn equipment as well as a buggy on his way home. He turned into the long, newly rocked lane that led to the log cabin he and Skye were completing.

He'd always dreamed of living in a log cabin, and Skye had

gotten all excited when he suggested it. It'd been her idea to approach her grandfather about buying a plot of land from him, and the pieces fell into place. They still had some finish work to do, like putting on the cabinet handles that he'd picked up at Wellsford Hardware. But for the most part, their new home was completed, and they loved it.

Bo rolled his Harley to a stop near the back door, and noticed that Skye had started planting some flowers while he was gone. The garden spade and three flats of flowers were lying on the ground near the deck, and several plants stood in the dirt, looking small and fragile.

Skye was inside, he heard, as he stepped through the back door. She was talking on the phone, and her voice sounded strained and tense. He walked into the kitchen to find Skye pacing the floor, listening to whoever was on the other end of the phone connection. He wondered who it could be, and then he knew.

"I didn't say I didn't want you to come for a visit. I just said I hope you'll feel comfortable around here—especially since you couldn't make yourself come to the wedding," Skye's words dripped with bitterness, and Bo hurt for his wife, and for the person hearing her words—her biological mother.

"I know, I know, everybody would have stared at you. Look, Andrea—Mom—I'm sorry I brought it up. Sure you can come see us. Just let us know when, and we'll pick you up at the airport."

Skye listened again, and then said, "Yeah, I know. See you soon. Bye!"

She clicked the phone off, set it down on the table, and looked at Bo.

"She's coming here," Skye said flatly, "in about three weeks."

"I gathered that," Bo answered, reaching for Skye. "Honey, it'll be okay. Maybe it won't be easy, but in the long run, it'll be okay."

"I guess so. It's just that she was too scared of what people would say about her to come to my wedding—the most wonderful day of my life. It's hard for me to forget that. I should have learned by now—she can't force herself to show up at any of my life's important events—not my high school graduation, not when I had the transplant, not at Angela's funeral, and not at my wedding. She made it to my birth, but she didn't stay long," Skye chuckled darkly at her joke. "I should be used to this by now."

"But she has been in touch with you off and on, and she wants to see you now," Bo tried to reason with Skye.

"Yeah, I can hardly wait," Skye muttered, and began walking out the door. "I'd better get my flowers in so the place is pretty for my *mother* when she comes."

Bo sighed deeply. What would ever erase the years of pain and bitterness Skye harbored in her heart against the mother who had left her behind at birth?

Several days later, Bo noticed Jonas working in the garden when he drove past the farm on his way home from work. A sudden inspiration hit him, and he swung his Harley onto the yard. The old man looked up from his stooped position and waved at Bo, then slowly began walking toward him.

"Danke, danke, danke," he said in Pennsylvania Dutch, his blue eyes twinkling under his straw hat. "I needed a reason to stop that endless weeding. Thank you for saving me from spending eternity in that garden."

Bo laughed. "I'm thinking you wouldn't mind spending eternity in a garden, if you didn't have to do any weeding."

"Ah, you're right about that. Seems like that was the plan all along, until Adam and Eve messed it up for the rest of us," Jonas shook his head. "Let's go get us some tea and sit on the porch."

Sue Ann greeted Bo warmly when he and Jonas entered the kitchen, and he realized, like he had before, how much love and security emanated from this home. It was no wonder Skye had such wonderful memories of times spent with her grandparents as a child, and why she had suggested settling down near them.

Sue Ann poured them glasses of freshly brewed mint garden tea, and sent a plate of cookies to the porch with them as well. Bo didn't waste any time broaching the subject with Jonas that had made him stop at the farm a few moments earlier.

"Skye got a call from her biological mother a few days ago," he began, and Jonas looked at him with interest. "She wants to come visit us in about three weeks. What bothers me is how bitter Skye still is toward Andrea. Is there anything we can do—anybody can do—to help her get over that?"

Jonas chewed his cookie and took a sip of tea, then he answered slowly. "I think, Bo, that the only person who can do that is Skye. It's called forgiveness. She has to forgive Andrea for the past and be willing to start anew. It's a hard thing to do."

Both men were quiet for awhile. The clop-clop-clop of an approaching horse and buggy filled the stillness, and when the buggy went by, Jonas said, "Phyllis Petershiem. Probably going home from a hen party."

Bo chuckled. He knew enough to know that a hen party was when a group of Amish women met in a home to quilt together. What he didn't understand was how Jonas knew one buggy from another—they all looked the same to him.

"How do you know?" he asked.

"I know the horse, and I know the buggy, and I know Phyllis," Jonas smiled.

"But the horses and the buggies all look the same, and I could hardly see the person inside," Bo wouldn't give up easily.

"It comes from living here," Jonas said. "Give yourself a few years, and you'll know too."

"That reminds me. The other day I met Ezra Yoder in the Hardware Store, and the first thing he said to me was something about my wife not growing up with her real parents. It kinda caught me off guard. Why do you think he would ask something like that?"

Jonas's brow furrowed as he reached for another cookie. "I really don't know," he said. "As you get to know Ezra, you may find that he has some strange ways about him. He's a good man, but he isn't easy to understand. He's probably just curious—you may find the Amish being curious about you and Skye because you're different than us, and it gives us something to talk about," Jonas's eyes laughed at Bo. "I tried to warn you about that when you asked to buy some land to build your house."

"You're absolutely right, Jonas, you did." Bo grinned.

BO
FIVE

DESPITE SPENDING his entire life in the Wheat State, Bo had to admit he knew very little about the production and harvest of the golden crop. But then, he was in the majority in his ignorance, for a very small percentage of the residents of Kansas were involved in farming. And that percentage was a lot less than it had been several decades ago. Communities that in the past had retained many of their young people to carry on the farming tradition were now losing sons and daughters to urban employment, and the farming was carried on by a few large operators.

Except for the Wellsford community. Wellsford was different because its Amish population continued to flourish as small farmers. Despite the fact that none of them attended school beyond the eighth grade, they knew how to make the most of their resources, how to farm efficiently, how to supplement their farm income with cottage industries, and how to keep their young folks at home. The Amish faith, tradition, working the land, and living a simple conservative lifestyle—these elements intertwined to bind the people together in ways that outsiders found intriguing and hard to understand.

Bo was one of those outsiders. But for one week in June, he found himself submersed in the culture of wheat and the Amish. It was a week he would never forget.

Every day, as soon as he got home from the Harley shop he owned in Vicksburg, he hurried to the farmstead Jonas and Sue Ann shared with their daughter Emma and her husband, Caleb. There he asked which field the harvesters were working in, and headed in that direction on his Harley. His job, when he got there, was to take wagon loads of wheat to town, pulling the wooden box wagon with a bordering-on-antique International tractor.

The first time he waited in line at the Wellsford Co-op grain elevator, he felt stupid. It happened to be a time when the only other vehicles in line were trucks—huge 600-bushel hauling trucks. And there he sat with his 60-bushel wagon. People expected that from the Amish, but they surely wondered who this "English" man was with the Amish equipment.

Interestingly enough, there were three groups of Amish in the community—something he'd learned when he asked Jonas why they farmed with tractors and other Amish still used horses. Jonas had told Bo that when he was young, there was only one group, and they all farmed with horses. But then, just before he and Sue Ann got married, the community had split over the horses-versus-tractors issue, and the more progressive group left and switched to tractors. Sue Ann's parents were part of that group. Jonas's parents had stayed with the group that believed tractors were a big step in the direction of "the world" that shouldn't be taken. Forced to choose which Amish church to belong to, Jonas and Sue Ann finally opted for the Horses group.

"But what does that have to do with religion?" Bo had dared to ask the old Amish minister recounting the story for him.

"I'm afraid nothing at all, in my opinion," Jonas had admitted. "But some traditions are worth keeping if they keep us humble and living simply."

Jonas had gone on to explain that just within the last few years, the issue of horses and tractors had come up again in his own church. It was getting more and more difficult to make a living with horses, the farmers had complained. This time, Jonas had felt led to agree with them. The question was brought to a vote within the congregation—a vote that would have to pass with 100 percent approval for the change to take place. It did, but only because the ten families who were known to oppose the change had opted to meet separately that morning, thus beginning a new church group.

"It's makes me sad, but that's the way our church constitution is set up," Jonas said. "We can't have communion until we all agree, and so the other option is to split."

Bo didn't know if he was more or less confused after that discussion. He just knew that he was driving a tractor to town—not a team of horses, and not a big truck.

And he got used to it. People soon knew who he was, and began initiating conversations with him while they waited to dump their grain.

By the second evening, Bo knew what to do and was having a great time. Granted, he wasn't an expert at backing the tractor up to the wagon full of wheat and matching the tractor hitch to the wagon tongue, but he was getting better. He enjoyed the slow drive of several miles into Wellsford, partly for the same reason he enjoyed riding a motorcycle—the outdoors was so close and intimate. No fabricated shell around him providing protection from the sun and surrounding him with a climate-controlled environment—no, he liked being out there, soaking up the world with all of his senses.

His trip to town that second evening, right after sunset, might end up in a song someday, he figured. The words weren't all together yet, but they'd come. Words to paint the picture of a windmill silhouette, black against a brilliant red-orange sky. Words for the motorized humming of combines in one field, and the instinctive humming of cicadas in the trees. Words to describe the smell of dirt and grease on his hands, and the field of freshly spread manure. Words to name the welcome taste of cold water in the Coleman jug that traveled with him on the tractor.

The trip that evening seemed short, and Bo soon found himself in the line, waiting to unload, talking to the young Amish boy with a team of horses in front of him. The kid was as brown as he could be, and his ever-present straw hat, barn-door pants and light cotton shirt did nothing to distinguish him from any of the other boys in the community. But Bo remembered seeing his face, and he remembered seeing him the evening before. The words Jonas had said came back and made Bo smile. "It comes from living here. Give yourself a few years, and you'll know too." A week of wheat harvest would surely give him a great start.

※ ※ ※

The next afternoon, when he arrived at the field, Bo sensed immediately that Caleb was on edge. In his early 40's, the stocky Amishman's mouth was set in a firm line above his brown beard, and his hurried movements made Bo nervous immediately. Had something happened? What was bothering him?

"Get this load into town and hurry right back," Caleb said. "It's fixin' to storm. Maybe hail."

Bo had noticed the cloud bank in the west on his way home, and the thought had crossed his mind that it looked like rain. But hail? Hail meant disaster. Hail meant the destruction of a year's worth of time, money and hope for a harvest. What made Caleb think it was going to hail?

He posed the question, yelling it at Caleb's retreating back as he ran for his tractor and combine. Caleb turned momentarily, gestured at the sky, and hollered something Bo couldn't hear. Then Caleb was on the tractor, pulling the combine, forcing the golden wheat into its throat. Bo jumped on his tractor, put it in gear, and pulled the wagon full of wheat out of the field and onto the road.

He watched the clouds the whole way to Wellsford. He didn't have the years of weather-watching expertise the Amish came by naturally—his weather information came to him from radar, relayed by radio and TV personnel. He wished so much for a radio on the tractor right now, but of course there wasn't any. The Amish didn't have such worldly conveniences. The dark-blue cloud bank was high enough now that some cars approaching him had their lights on, and that made him realize how ominous things really were looking. The previous day's joy of driving the cabless tractor was fading as fast as the daylight, and he wanted desperately to reach Wellsford and dump his wheat before the storm hit.

The wind picked up as he turned into the driveway of the Co-op. He shuddered, but not from cold—it had to be at least 95 degrees. The chill inside of him originated somewhere in the clouds above him—clouds that resembled hard puffs of cotton. Hail clouds.

The inevitable line of trucks, tractors, and teams of horses was waiting outside the elevator. No way would they all be able to unload their grain before the deluge hit. If only he had a tarp to put over the wagon. But he didn't.

The raindrops began slowly. A big splat here, and another there. Then, without warning, the clouds opened the floodgates, and like water cascading over a dam, sheets of rain swept across the yard. Bo jumped from the tractor and sprinted into the huge elevator doors. He was soaked.

Several other men and women who'd been driving tractors were also inside the elevator, dripping wet, staring at the downpour. He could hardly see through the rain, but Bo knew there were several people out there who'd had to stay with their horses. The little Amish kid was probably one of them. The rain was bad, but what if. . .

It came even as Bo thought the word. Like the rain, slowly,

with a few small ice balls at first. Then more, and larger. Like cold, noisy golfballs, the hail crashed onto the ground, bounced off trucks and tractors, and terrorized the horses. Several men ran out of the elevator to try to help hold the horses. Bo's stomach knotted and his mouth turned dry as he watched in frozen fear.

One of the teams broke, charging past the elevator doors and down the street. Bo caught a glimpse of a small body falling, and the wagon rolling over it. He ran out into the hail and rain.

BO
SIX

He hated hospitals. They had that smell to them. And they were full of people in various stages of crisis, and he didn't like that either. If anything scared him about marrying Skye, it was that someday he'd have to see her in the hospital. As long as she managed her diabetes and took care of herself, she should be okay. But you never knew. . .

"And you never know when you're gonna get hit on your cycle and banged up big time," Skye had said when he confessed his fear to her. "So we're just gonna have to take our risks with each other."

But it was somebody else's trauma that brought him to the emergency waiting room this evening. The little Amish boy had been unconscious when he picked him up outside the elevator, and one leg hung loosely at a very wrong angle. An ambulance rushed him to the Vicksburg Hospital while one of the Co-op employees drove to the boy's family to let them know and take them to the hospital.

The storm had lasted about fifteen minutes, and then Bo, along with the others in the line at the elevator, unloaded their soaked wheat onto the hail-strewn ground. Tension had been heavy among the farmers—they wanted to get back to their fields to see if the hail had hit them. Bo had wondered himself what had happened to Caleb's fields, and as he left Wellsford, he began to hope against hope that what he saw wouldn't greet him back at the farm.

Sitting in the waiting room, Bo could still see the picture in his mind. Fields of wheat that had swayed tall and proud on his way into Wellsford were now stripped. Stripped of their grain, stripped of their value, stripped of all that mattered to the farmers. Broken and bent, the wheat stalks stood alone, their heads crushed by the hail. Bo ached inside, and knew it was a black day for the Wellsford community.

But wheat could be planted again. What mattered now was the life of that Amish kid in the emergency room. The son of Ezra Yoder, he'd found out.

The Co-op manager had brought Ezra and his wife to the hospital, but at least one of them would be needing a ride home. Bo had volunteered to do that, but he wasn't sure why. Maybe it was because he'd been there when the accident happened, and held the listless boy in his arms. Maybe because he was as intrigued with getting to know the Amish as Ezra seemed to be curious about Skye's background. For whatever reason, Bo was there at the hospital, waiting.

It seemed to take forever, and Bo was not one to sit quietly and wait. He wished he'd picked up Skye and brought her along, rather than calling to tell her he was going. He paced. Picked up a magazine. Put it down. Picked up another one.

Finally, Ezra emerged from one of the rooms and walked toward Bo. Bo tried to read the face of the tall lanky Amishman, but couldn't.

"Doc says he had a concussion, and he's coming out of it," Ezra said. "They'll be taking him into surgery to fix that leg—it's banged up pretty bad."

"But he's going to be okay," Bo half-questioned, half-stated.

"Yah, I think so."

❧ ❧ ❧

Ten-year-old Cris Yoder was going to be all right, but his badly broken leg was going to keep him in the hospital for at least a week. His parents and other family members would need rides back and forth from Vicksburg—an hour's drive by car. They could hire an "Amish taxi"—a person in the community who hauled the Amish for a fee. But that would get expensive, and, as Bo and Skye talked about it, maybe this was one opportunity for them to help their neighbors. So they offered their services, saying that Bo could take anyone into Vicksburg in the morning when he went to work, and bring them back in the afternoon, or Skye was available to drive them as well at other times.

One evening, a week after the accident, Ezra stopped in around 8:00 and asked if someone could take him to see Cris and bring his wife, Lizzie, home, who'd been there all day. Bo, who was in the middle of a fence-building project, looked at Skye.

"I don't think Bo wants to leave his fence," Skye said to the Amishman standing in the yard next to his horse and hack buggy. "So I'd be glad to take you—I can go get some groceries at Mid-Kansas Discount while I'm there."

Skye left with Ezra, and Bo lost himself in building a fence for the sheep that he and Skye planned to buy as soon as possible. "Lawn mowers that give natural fertilizer and lambs that make money" was how Jonas had described sheep when he suggested that Bo and Skye acquire several head. Neither of them had any experience with the critters, but both were willing to give it a try.

It was late when Skye returned, and Bo had fallen asleep on the couch in front of the TV. He woke up when the door slammed.

Skye came in and sat down on the floor beside the couch, her face even with Bo's. "Hi, honey," he said, yawning. "I fell asleep."

"I see that," she replied, tracing his dark eyebrows with her finger. Her forefinger traveled down his nose, around his lips, and up across both cheeks. Bo closed his eyes, absorbing her soft touch. Then the feeling was different, for it was her mouth following the same journey across his face. Amazing what a little nap and a woman can do for a man's energy, he chuckled deep in his throat.

He returned her kisses, and at some point Skye said she needed to tell him about Ezra, but it could wait until morning. Bo agreed. Ezra could wait.

❧ ❧ ❧

They sat together on the deck the next morning, eating the waffles Bo had made. They loved to share breakfast on the deck during the summer—if they got up at 5:30, they could enjoy a leisurely meal as they watched and listened to the world wake up, and Bo could still make it to the shop by 8:00. This morning he was eager to hear what Skye had to say about Ezra.

"The man is strange," Skye began as she poured syrup over her waffle. "We were barely off his yard when he began asking me questions about my birth, my 'real' mother and father, if I know who they are, if I ever see them—all that kind of stuff. I didn't want to be rude, but I didn't know why I should be telling those things to a man I hardly know."

"What did you say?"

"Just the basics. And then I tried to change the subject. I managed to get him on sheep for awhile—he has a herd, you know. That worked for awhile. But then he'd come back to it. He asked me if it was hard for me to find my parents."

"I don't understand it either," Bo said, sipping his coffee. "Why is he so curious about your background?"

"I haven't a clue. He's a nice enough guy, but to be honest, I'll be glad when Cris is home and I don't have to take Ezra to Vicksburg anymore."

"It shouldn't be much longer. What'd they say last night?"
"A few more days."

&? &? &?

Skye's biological mother, Andrea, had said she'd be there for a visit "about three weeks" after she called. She called again when the three weeks were nearly up, and said she'd be flying in on July 15. Bo knew Skye hated the delay, but the 15th finally arrived, and so did Andrea.

The short, petite woman in her early 50's walked out of the airline's ramp, into the airport, and toward Bo and Skye, a trembling smile on her face. She hugged Skye, then Bo, then Skye again. They walked to the baggage claim, making small talk.

Bo had never seen Andrea before, and he found his first impressions colliding with the things Skye had told him about her. He saw a friendly face, the same luminous green eyes he loved in Skye, and short red hair. She seemed warm and approachable—not the mother whom Skye accused of avoiding all of the important events of her life. Still, those were the facts. He hoped the time that they'd spend together over the next week would bring them together.

They spent the hour's drive from Vicksburg to their home talking about the Amish, their new house, and Andrea's life in Florida. She was recently divorced, and working as the manager of a motel.

Bo knew everyone was avoiding talking about the wedding, but he also knew Skye. She wouldn't ignore it for long. She would need to clear the air with her mother, and it would happen sooner rather than later.

It came later that evening. The three of them were sitting on the deck, sipping drinks and watching the lightning bugs flit across the yard. Andrea remarked on how quiet it was in the country compared to her condominium, and Skye said that was one reason why they'd decided to live there.

They were quiet for awhile, and Bo could feel the tension. He knew both women were afraid to talk about the real issues between them, and yet both knew they had to. Skye finally broke the silence.

"I appreciate you coming to visit," she began. "And I'm sorry if I sounded strange about it when we talked on the phone. It's just that I can't seem to get over the fact that. . .that you've missed so much of my life up until now. . .including our wedding."

Andrea stood up and walked to the edge of the deck. She took a sip from the glass in her hand, and then slowly turned to face her daughter seated on one of the redwood deck chairs.

"Skye, I have made many mistakes in my life. The first one might have been leaving you and Angela after you were born, but I'm not sure that was a mistake. You were raised in a wonderful home by great parents—and that's more than I could have given you.

"Coming to your graduation but not seeing you then—that was probably a mistake. But I was scared—scared I'd mess up the life you had, and scared you'd be mad at me.

"Not getting to know Angela before she died—that was a horrible mistake," Andrea said, and Bo heard a catch in her voice. "I can't forgive myself for that. This has been a bad year for me, because I've felt so guilty and ashamed."

"And that's why I couldn't make myself come to your wedding, as much as I wanted to be there. I was afraid of all the people who would be whispering about me, knowing that I was the mother who gave you up and wasn't involved in your life. Plus, I didn't want to ruin it for you and your parents. I didn't want to bring extra stress to what should be your perfect day."

Bo heard Skye sigh loudly beside him as she shifted in the chair, but she didn't say anything. She had obviously decided to let her mother talk as long as she wanted to without interruption.

"But I want more than anything else to begin a relationship with you—something I tried but couldn't do a year ago, after Angela died. I've been in counseling this year. I've worked through the grief, and I'm working on the guilt. Coming to see you is part of that process. Skye, honey, please help me."

Andrea moved toward Skye, and Bo watched as Skye stood up and gave her mother the hug that Andrea obviously needed and wanted. Andrea was crying, but as Skye looked over her mother's shoulder at Bo, he could see that her eyes were dry.

SKYE

SKYE
ONE

The getting out of bed was the hard part. Usually she and Bo got up at the same time to eat breakfast together, and then she'd go for her walk after Bo went to work. But this was Sunday. Bo was taking the opportunity to sleep in a bit, and her mother was there, so they'd all eat breakfast around 8:00, then go to church. Skye could have slept in too, but she needed the walk—emotionally more than physically.

So when the alarm sounded at 6:00, Skye clicked it off and tried not to think about how nice it would be to stay in bed with Bo. She slipped on a pair of shorts, a T-shirt with the sleeves cut out of it, socks and walking shoes. It looked like a beautiful morning.

Skye stepped out onto the deck and went through her stretching exercises. Then she followed their newly rocked lane to the road, and turned right.

It really was the best part of the day to be outdoors in the summer and she loved it, now that she was out here. The sun had been up for about a half hour, and it promised to bake the landscape that day. The temperature would climb from the 80 degrees she'd seen on the thermometer on the deck, and by afternoon it'd probably top 100. Yes, she was glad to be walking now.

Skye recognized the lilting song of a meadowlark somewhere

nearby, and spotted him on a fence post along the road. He took wing as she strode past, and she envied his carefree life. Maybe meadowlarks had their problems too, but this morning he seemed free, and she felt all tied up in knots.

The talk with her mother the evening before should have made her feel good. Andrea had admitted making mistakes, feeling guilty and ashamed. She said she wanted to work on her relationship with Skye. She'd been sorry about the past, and wanted to look toward the future. Skye should have been happy to hear her words.

Well, the words were fine and good, Skye churned, and her stride reflected her anger. But for 35 years she'd missed the actions, and she couldn't just forget it. She couldn't say, "Oh, that's okay, Mom," because it wasn't. The words she felt like saying screamed inside of her: "You came to our graduation and talked to Dad but didn't show up at our party. But I'll forget how cheated I felt. It's okay that you never knew what a wonderful person Angela was. She died not knowing you either, but that's in the past. Sure, let's go on from here, when there's only one of us left."

Skye felt the anger at her biological mother and at Angela's untimely death spill out into tears, and she hoped she wouldn't meet anyone on the road. This early on a Sunday, no one should be out. She let herself cry, and then wished she'd thought to bring a handkerchief along. She sniffled and wiped at her eyes.

She came to the intersection between two county roads and turned south. Her grandparents lived a half mile down this road. They'd be going to church today too—sitting in a hot, stuffy house for three hours on backless benches, without any air-conditioning or even fans to move the air around. And for an hour of that time, her grandfather would be standing and preaching to the congregation. She wondered what he would talk about— what message would he share "off the top of his head" without any notes, with only his Bible in his hand.

When Skye reached the farmstead, she could hear the diesel engine of the milking machine out in the dairy barn, and knew Caleb, Emma and their children were doing the morning chores. Then she noticed her grandfather sitting on a rocking chair on the porch, his Bible in his lap. He seemed to have fallen asleep. Probably been up a while already, Skye surmised, and she continued her power-walking past the farm.

She walked to the next intersection, and then turned to retrace her steps. This time, as she drew near the farm, she saw her grandfather standing on the porch, watching her. She knew she'd better stop to say hi.

"Good morning, Dawdi," she said, using the Pennsylvania Dutch word for grandfather—the only name she'd ever used for her Amish grandfather.

"Good morning, Skye. You're out early today!" the old man's face crinkled with a smile above his white beard.

"Yeah, I decided to go before breakfast—maybe if I'm lucky Bo and Andrea will have it ready when I get home!" Skye smiled.

"That's right, your natural mother is here—when did she come?"

"Yesterday."

"How's it going?"

What should she say? "Okay, I guess."

Skye felt Jonas's bright blue eyes study her face, and she knew he read much more inside of her than he heard in her words.

"I hope it will be okay, Skye. Come over sometime. Soon. Bring your hamonica—I'd like to hear you play."

"Oh, I'm not very good."

"Then come sing for me. I know you're good at that."

Skye laughed. "Okay, Dawdi, I'll come sing for you."

"Soon?"

"Sure, soon. But now I have to get home."

❦ ❦ ❦

Skye had been a regular church attender for half of her life so far—the first half. The half when she was still under the wings of her Mennonite parents in Pennsylvania. But when she graduated from high school and moved to New York to pursue her singing career, her connection with church and, to a great extent, with God drifted far into the background. She had bigger and better things to do, it seemed at the time.

The death of her twin sister jerked Skye into a new reality. Like a young calf lassoed around the neck and thrown to the ground at a Kansas rodeo, Skye's feet disappeared from under her. Her stability had always been Angela. Consistent, ever-present, ever-helping and loving Angela. Even when Skye took to the road as a rock performer and Angela married an Iowa farmer, they kept in touch. Angela was always there for Skye.

And then suddenly she wasn't—a blow that at first found Skye screaming at God, then weeping, and finally walking in a new relationship with her Creator. It was this newfound faith that brought her and Bo to the Wellsford Mennonite Church when they moved to Kansas.

They went to church that hot July morning, and Andrea was with them. It'd be the first time anyone in Wellsford would see her mother, and both women were nervous.

The red brick church building near the center of town had a congregation of approximately 150 people. Skye and Bo had felt welcome immediately when they began to attend. Pastor Marge was a big part of that, but so were the other church members.

After talking briefly to some of the people gathered in the foyer, Skye was relieved when they were seated. Maybe Andrea had been right after all about the wedding—introducing her biological mother to her friends was harder than she'd thought, and she could feel the uneasiness in the woman beside her.

Pastor Marge stood in front of them, welcoming the congregation and visitors to the worship service. She smiled directly at the trio seated in the fourth row, and Skye smiled back. Thankfully, Pastor Marge didn't mention any names or ask Andrea to stand, as she often did. *She knows this is tough*, Skye realized.

Skye relaxed as they sang several hymns, and one of the men from the congregation told the children's story. Someone else read the Scripture passage, and then Pastor Marge stood up to give the sermon.

"I have a story to tell you this morning," she began. "It's about a well-known set of twins." Skye's heart jumped at the last word, and then she heard Marge continue. "Jacob and Esau. As you heard in the Scripture, these twin sons of Isaac and Rebekah were very different. Esau was a big, tough, macho kind of guy who loved to hunt—an outdoorsman. Jacob was just the opposite—he was quiet, stayed inside a lot, and helped his mother around the tent. As you might guess, that made him his mother's favorite, while Isaac liked Esau.

"Fortunately for Isaac, the son he liked best was also born first, which meant that Isaac would give him a special blessing. When it came time to do that, Rebekah schemed with her favorite son to get the blessing for him instead.

"Esau was a hairy man, and Isaac was almost blind in his old age, and those two things together helped Jacob and his mother pull off the trick. She put some goat skins on Jacob's smooth hands and face, and dressed him in Esau's clothes, so when he went in to see Isaac, he felt and smelled like his brother Esau.

"Now you've gotta give the old man some credit—he was suspicious. He'd told Esau to go hunting, then cook the game and bring it to him. They would have a feast together, and Isaac would give Esau the blessing. When Jacob showed up with food that Rebekah had made for him to take in, Isaac wanted to know how Esau could be back so soon. Jacob lied, and said it was because God helped him hunt it quickly. Isaac still wasn't convinced, because the man talking to him sounded like Jacob, not Esau. So he asked to touch him, and that's when Rebekah's creativity paid off. Jacob was a temporarily hairy guy.

"Isaac didn't know what to think. The man in front of him sounded like Jacob and felt like Esau. 'Are you really my son Esau?' he asked. Jacob lied again and said he was.

"'Then come kiss me,' Isaac said, and when Jacob did, Isaac smelled the outdoors on his clothes and believed it was his son Esau. And he proceeded to give him the all-important blessing that went to the firstborn son.

"Well, Jacob had no more than left the room and gone to his mother to celebrate their successful deceit when the real Esau showed up. It didn't take long for him and Isaac to figure out what happened.

"Talk about one angry man. We're not sure what all Esau said, but it included, 'I'm going to kill that Jacob.'"

Pastor Marge paused. Skye remembered the story from her childhood years in Sunday school, but she'd never heard it told like this from the pulpit.

"As you can imagine, Esau and Jacob go their separate ways," Pastor Marge continued. "Years and years go by—years that have their own very interesting things happening in them, and we'll talk about that on another Sunday. But for this morning, I want to fast-forward ahead to a time when Jacob, who's been gone from his homeland for a long time, decides he wants to go back. He's a rich man now with two wives, eleven children, and huge herds of livestock. He's rich, and he's scared to death. He's terrified that his brother will keep his promise to kill him when he shows up back at home.

"Now, rather than stealing from his brother, Jacob is into begging and bribing for mercy. His bribe looks something like this: 200 female goats and 20 male goats, 200 ewes and 20 rams,

30 camels and their colts, 40 cows and 10 bulls, 20 female donkeys and 10 male donkeys."

Pastor Marge smiled at the congregation. "Whether or not you're a farmer, I think you can see that Jacob was very sorry for what he'd done and quite serious about wanting forgiveness.

"Jacob sent all those animals ahead of him as a peace offering to Esau. Then he got up his nerve and began walking toward his brother, bowing himself to the ground seven times before he even got close.

"What do you think happened?

"Simply this: Esau *ran* out to meet Jacob, gave him the biggest hug in the world, and they cried together.

"When they were done crying, Esau admired Jacob's wives and children, and then he asked; 'So what's with all of that livestock you sent ahead of you?' Jacob said it was a gift from him in the hopes of finding favor with his brother. Esau said that was totally unnecessary—he didn't need Jacob's animals. Then Jacob said 'No, please, take my gift that I brought for you, because God has dealt graciously with me, and because I have everything I want.'"

Pastor Marge looked out over the congregation, her eyes searching the faces turned toward her.

"I tell that story this morning because there's not one of us here this morning who hasn't been wronged, dumped on, tricked, lied to or cheated in one way or another. We are all Esau's.

"At the same time, every one of us has done somebody wrong, been mean, tricked or lied to someone, violated the respect God wants us to have for each other. We are all Jacob's.

"Each one of us needs to seek forgiveness, and grant forgiveness. I'd like to end this message with some quiet time. Use this time to think about who you may need to forgive, or from whom you may need to seek forgiveness."

Pastor Marge sat down. Skye closed her eyes.

SKYE
TWO

S**KYE SAT MOTIONLESS** in the church pew, her eyes closed, her ears picking up the sounds of sniffling next to her. Her mother was crying. The forgiveness sermon was getting to her.

To be honest, Skye wished it would get to her too. She wished she could be an Esau. She wished she could forgive her mother, but she couldn't. At least not here, not now, in church, where everybody would see her and hear her bawling her head off. No, it wouldn't happen this morning.

Skye heaved a sigh of relief when Pastor Marge finally ended the time of silence with a prayer. Andrea was blowing her nose beside Skye, and Skye was embarrassed. She hated to admit it, but she was. For the next week, when people from the church talked about that morning's service, they'd say "Skye's real mother was there—the sermon on forgiveness really seemed to hit her hard."

She could see it on the faces of some of the people as they left the service that morning—sympathetic smiles thinly disguising curious stares. Not everyone, of course. Some really cared, and she was beginning to know who those were. The others. . . well, she'd grown up in a church and known that being Christian didn't seem to automatically make people nice, and this church was no different.

Skye, Bo and Andrea were walking to their car when one of the church members called out to them from the church doors, asking if they had plans for lunch. Skye looked at Bo, then at the couple about their age at the door. "No, not really," Skye answered.

"Why don't you join us for pizza—there's four of us families going," the woman said.

"Sure, sounds good—thanks!" Bo replied.

"If that's okay with you," Skye addressed Andrea, who nodded.

"I'd like to meet some of your church friends," she said.

& & &

That evening, around 8:00, a horse and buggy drove into Bo and Skye's yard and stopped in front of the log cabin. Bo, Skye and Andrea had settled in with bowls of popcorn, chips and cheese dip for an evening of videos when they heard the buggy roll in. Bo went to the door and opened it.

"Well, hello Dawdi," Bo said, and Skye smiled. It still tickled her to hear Bo call her grandfather "Dawdi," a term he used interchangeably with "Jonas." "Come on in," Bo continued. "How did you know it was movie night at our house?"

Skye could hear Jonas chuckling as he made his way slowly toward the house. "Ah, Bo, you know I could hear that worldly TV all the way to my house, and I had to come see what was showing," Jonas stepped inside the house. He took off his straw hat and nodded at Skye and her mother. "Hello, Skye. And this must be your mother."

"Yes, I'm Andrea." Andrea stood up from where she was sitting on the couch and reached out to shake Jonas's hand. "I'm very pleased to meet you."

"It's good to meet you too," Jonas said, his bright blue eyes taking in the petite red-haired woman. "You have a very special daughter."

"I know," Andrea said. "But I don't know her as well as you

do. I hope to work on that during this next week."

"I wish you both the best," Jonas said, his gaze moving from Andrea to Skye. He paused, his attention caught by the scene on the TV screen, and Skye smiled to herself. Inevitably, the TV always grabbed the Amish, since they weren't allowed to have them in their homes.

"Anyway, I was on my way to check the cows in the Frey pasture, and Sue Ann said I should stop by and invite you all to supper tomorrow," Jonas said, breaking away from the television. "Can you come?"

"Can we come?" Bo answered. "Can we show up for some of the best food in the country? What do you think, Skye and Andrea?"

Skye grinned at her grandfather, anticipating the meal her grandmother would have ready for them. "Yes, Dawdi, I think we can be there. Thanks a lot!"

"Good! And now I have one more question," Jonas said, and Skye saw him looking directly at her. "I'm wondering if you have time to come check the cows with me this evening. I know you're in the middle of some very important movies, but I have something important to talk to you about too."

Skye's curiosity piqued. What could Dawdi want? She looked at Bo and her mother, and saw the questions in her mind reflected in their eyes. "I can't say no to an offer like that," she said. "You know I'm dying of curiosity, Dawdi."

"Let's go then," Jonas said, turning toward the door. "I'll take good care of her, Bo," his eyes twinkled.

"I'm not at all worried," Bo answered.

Skye followed the old Amish man as he slowly made his way out the door, down the steps of the front porch, and to his horse. He untied the big bay mare while Skye climbed up into the open buggy, then she watched as Jonas lifted himself onto the seat beside her. He took the reins in his wrinkled hands and clicked his tongue at the horse. The mare turned around in the yard and trotted dutifully down the lane.

Skye wondered how long it would be before Jonas brought up what he wanted to talk about. She had never in her life felt uncomfortable around Dawdi, and tonight was no exception. Still, the element of the unknown topic hung between them, and it made her just a little bit nervous.

"How'd it go with your mother today?" Jonas asked when they reached the end of the lane and turned onto the sand road.

Skye let the clop-clop-clop of the mare's steady gait fill the silence as she contemplated her answer. She could say "Okay" and leave it at that. Or she could mention Pastor Marge's sermon that morning, and how she knew she should forgive her mother, but just couldn't, somehow. She knew Dawdi would be a good person to talk to, when she was ready. But she wasn't ready. Not yet.

"Okay," she answered noncommitally. "She went to church with us, and the people didn't stare too much. In fact, we went out for lunch with some people from church, and that was okay too. Maybe I can get used to having my 'other mother' around."

"I hope so, Skye." Jonas said. "I want to tell you what happened to me this morning."

Skye turned to look at Dawdi, but he was staring straight.

"This morning I was sitting on the porch, reading my Bible, and I guess I dozed off a little bit. I'd been thinking about the sermon for this morning, and when I fell asleep, I dreamed about something I'd just read. It was the story of Peter denying Christ. I dreamed I was there, watching it happen. It made me so angry, to see Peter do that. And then I saw Christ, and I heard him say 'Peter, you are the rock on which I am going to build my church.' I couldn't believe Christ would say that, after what Peter did to him. I was still angry at Peter, and then I woke up, and I saw you walking down the road."

Jonas paused, and a memory began sifting into Skye's mind. It hadn't been many years ago—not even two. But in life experiences, it felt like a century away.

She remembered being at a party after one of her rock concerts—the last party before the kidney transplant. She'd gotten drunk. So drunk that when someone at the party said he'd seen a woman that looked just like her at a church convention, and asked her if she by any chance had a twin sister, she'd said no. No! She'd denied having a twin! She'd been so drunk and so embarrassed at her behavior that she couldn't admit she had a sister named Angela—a good and beautiful sister.

The next day Angela came to pick her up and take her to Iowa for the kidney transplant. The only way Skye had been able to face her was to bury the denial deep in her mind, and hope it would never come back again.

And now it had.

Skye buried her head in her hands as she sat in the buggy next to her grandfather, and she allowed the emotions to pour out. She cried for her denial, and she cried for never telling Angela. She cried because she knew if she had told Angela, her sister would have been hurt, but she would also have forgiven Skye immediately. She cried because she had never been able to forgive herself for that incident, or for the lifestyle that led to her kidney failure. She sobbed shoulder-shaking sobs for the death of a sister—a death she felt partially responsible for.

"I. . .I did that to Angela once," she said to Jonas, realizing he was probably wondering about her sudden outburst. Then she went on to tell him the story. By the time she was done, the buggy they were sitting in was parked alongside the pasture fence.

"If we walk up to the top of the hill, we'll probably be able to see the cows," Jonas said, getting down from the buggy. He tied the mare's lead rope to the fence post, and then Skye followed him through the gate into the pasture.

"You told me about your dream, and then I started bawling," Skye said as they dodged the big brown cow pies in the grass. "But

I don't think you've told me everything you wanted to, have you?"

"No, but the interruption was good. I think you needed that."

Skye didn't know what to say, so she just kept walking, her eyes to the ground.

"After the dream, and after you stopped to talk, and after you went on your way this morning, my heart was heavy," Jonas continued. "The most important thing about Peter's story was not his denial, but the fact that Jesus forgave him and made him the cornerstone of the Christian church. After seeing you and knowing how you feel about your mother, my heart was burdened, knowing that what she needs is your forgiveness. And she's not the only one who needs it—you need to forgive her so you can go on with your life. You will never have peace in your heart until you do."

They had reached the top of the slight incline. Ahead of them, on the side of the hill they couldn't see from the buggy, Jonas's small herd of thirteen black Angus cows grazed with contented purpose, all headed in the same direction. Behind them, the rays of the sun already set continued to play in the clouds. The scene in front of her began to blur, and Skye knew it was time. Here, in the open space she loved, with one of the people she trusted most in her life, she would quit fighting. There had to be a reason that Pastor Marge's sermon and Dawdi's words to her were all about forgiveness, all in the same day. It was time, and she was ready.

"What shall I do?" she asked as the tears began again.

"How about if you tell me, one at a time, the things you need to forgive your mother for. After each one, say, 'I forgive you, Mother.' Take a little while for it to sink in, and then go on."

And so she did, one by one.

An hour passed. It grew dark. The stars filled the Kansas sky with pinpricks of light. Jonas and Skye sat on top of the hill, the bearded old Amish man listening, the blonde-haired woman shedding years of bitterness.

They hardly noticed a car stop alongside the road, but then, in the distance, they heard familiar voices calling their names. "Bo and my mother are looking for us," Skye said, reaching for her grandfather in the dark. "Here, let me help you up."

They met Bo and Andrea's flashlight beam and then soon Bo and Andrea themselves, who were full of questions. Did they have problems? Were they okay?

"We're fine," Skye answered. "In fact, I'm really, really okay."

Skye fell in step with her birth mother and they walked arm-in-arm toward the pasture gate.

"Amazing what checking the cows with you can do to a person," Bo whispered to Jonas beside him.

"We're gonna have to thank God for this one," Jonas replied. "The cows were just there."

SKYE
THREE

Skye couldn't remember when she'd ever felt so free in her entire life. Sure, maybe as a child she'd known this kind of unrestricted joy in living. And certainly her life so far had included many happy times. But even in those, like her wedding, the pain of her birth mother's absence had lurked underneath, deep in her heart. She'd kept it buried much of the time, but when it surfaced, the grudge swamped her in bitterness.

Now the bad feelings against her mother were gone. She'd given them to God. She'd given her mother to God too. No longer did she have to carry the burden around of what she could do to make her mother "pay." It wasn't her problem anymore—it was between her mother and God. On the pasture hill that night, Skye had made a choice not to hold on to the bitterness and anger any more. And she'd prayed for healing in her relationship to her biological mother. Then, at Jonas's suggestion, she'd prayed for her mother Becca too. This would be a new experience for the woman who'd cared for her since she was born—the only mother she'd known until now. Skye didn't know how Becca would react to "sharing" her, but she knew it couldn't be easy.

The rest of the time with Andrea went so well that Skye began to wish her mother could stay longer. They had so much catching up to do! But Andrea had to get back to the motel she managed, so, a week after her arrival, Bo and Skye saw her off at the airport in Vicksburg. Bo and Skye said maybe they would visit her in Florida that winter, and Andrea said they could come and stay as long as they wanted—she'd give them a room at no cost. "Just come!" she pleaded, and Skye promised they would.

❧ ❧ ❧

The day after Andrea left, Skye was on the phone with her producer, Jake Jordan, talking about the next CD she was going to release, when she saw a horse and buggy coming down their lane. She could see from a distance it wasn't Jonas—it wasn't his horse, and it wasn't an old man driving. She wondered who it might be, but before long she recognized the tall Amish man. It was Ezra Yoder.

What would Ezra want? she wondered to herself as she listened to Jake carrying on about a new songwriter whose lyrics he thought Skye might be interested in. Skye watched as Ezra tied his horse up to the hitching post and approached the house. The doorbell rang, and she walked over to open it.

"You know I like to write my own lyrics," she told Jake, looking at Ezra standing on the porch in front of her. "Ezra, I'll be right there—I'm on the phone," she said.

"No problem. I can wait," Ezra said as he sat down on the front step.

Skye listened to Jake make his case for the newfound songwriter, and said sure she'd take a look at the lyrics, but she wouldn't make any promises. Jake said that's all he asked, and he'd e-mail them to her right away.

"So, what have you been doing to keep busy out there on that Kansas prairie?" the voice from New York continued. "Seen any tornadoes lately?"

"No, Jake, I haven't. Actually, I've got a visitor right now—an Amish guy. I need to go see what he wants—maybe we can talk more next time."

"Hey, may I never be accused of keeping an Amish man waiting—especially when he's there to see a good-looking woman like you," Jake laughed. "Have fun. Maybe he's there to take you for a spin in his buggy!"

"Jake, you are so strange," Skye laughed. "I'll talk to you later."

Skye clicked the cordless phone off and set it on the table, then walked out on the porch. She was suddenly conscious of the shirt and shorts she'd been wearing around the house—she hadn't expected anyone to drop in—certainly not Ezra Yoder. She could see his eyes travel up and down her body from where he was sitting, and she blushed.

"So, what brings you here, Ezra?" she asked. "You need a ride somewhere?"

"Nope. Came to talk about sheep," Ezra said, still sitting on the porch.

"Sheep?"

"Yah, you told me you were thinkin' about starting a herd."

"We have talked about it, yes." Skye felt strange standing on the porch looking down at Ezra, but he seemed in no hurry to stand up, so she sat down on the porch too, as far against her side as she could.

"I could help you get started," Ezra said. "I could sell you some ewes and a buck."

"We might be interested in that. I'll have to talk to Bo."

"You do that." Ezra paused, but made no effort to get up. "Your mother still here?"

"No, she went home yesterday," Skye answered, amazed and yet not surprised at all that he knew Andrea had been there.

"Doesn't she feel guilty about leaving you girls after you were born?"

Skye looked at Ezra, but he was staring straight ahead.

"I think she does," Skye replied slowly. "But she did the best she knew to do at the time, and that's all behind us now."

"Ain't you mad at her for doin' that?"

Skye had no idea why Ezra was asking these questions. He wasn't a complete stranger—they'd sort of gotten to know each other when she took him and his family to visit Cris in the hospital. But the questions seemed very personal, and she didn't know how to respond, especially if her answers were going to be fed into the community rumor mill.

At the same time, what did she have to hide? Her newfound freedom from bitterness felt so good, why not tell Ezra? He asked; he'd get his answer.

"Yes, I was angry at her for a long time, Ezra. But while she was here, I did something that changed everything. I asked God to forgive me for holding a grudge against her, and I promised God and myself not to be angry at her for those things anymore."

The Amish man beside her had nothing to say for a long time. Finally he stood up and looked down at Skye and into her eyes for the first time.

"If that works for you, that's good," he said. "Let me know if you want to buy some sheep."

Skye watched as Ezra sauntered toward his horse, untied him, and got into the buggy. He waved as he headed down the lane, and Skye shook her head. What a strange, strange man.

※ ※ ※

"He just showed up and wanted to talk about sheep?" Bo asked that evening when Skye told him about Ezra's unexpected visit.

"Well, I'm not sure if he wanted to talk about sheep or my relationship with my mother," Skye answered, setting the table for supper. She repeated her conversation with Ezra, and Bo stopped in the middle of cleaning out the dishwasher to listen. Skye could tell he was as baffled as she.

"And when you said all was forgiven and you'd put it behind

you, he didn't want to talk about it anymore?" Bo asked.

"Yep, he said if that works for me, great. And told me to let him know if we wanted to buy sheep. Then he left."

Bo shook his head, then a slow teasing smile spread across his handsome face. "I know what it is," he said, shaking a handful of silverware at Skye. "He's got the hots for you, and he's just making conversation to be around you. Yep, that's what it is."

Skye blushed involuntarily. She remembered the way Ezra had given her the once-over when she came out the door. She figured it was just a guy thing and she'd felt bad she'd been wearing skimpy clothes, by Amish standards. But she'd never thought of Ezra having ulterior motives.

"You don't really think so," she looked at Bo. "Ezra's married and surely he knows I am very happily married. He wouldn't. . ."

"Because he's Amish? Come on, Skye, Amish are people too. You are one beautiful woman. He can't help but have noticed that. But if he so much as dares to touch you. . ."

Bo's voice trailed off, and Skye knew all kidding was aside.

"He won't," she assured her husband. "He won't because I don't think that's what he wants, and it most certainly isn't what I want. I want *you*," Skye wrapped her arms around Bo from the back and nuzzled his neck. "You, you, and you."

"Good, because I'm not into sharing," Bo set the plate on the counter and turned toward his wife. "I'll buy *ewes* from Ezra, but he sure can't have *you!*"

"Oh, that's so cute, Bo," Skye kidded. "And is your last name Peep, and have you lost your sheep?"

Their laughter filled the log cabin, and Skye knew she had never been so happy.

🐑 🐑 🐑

Several days later, when Skye heard the clop-clop-clop of a horse's hooves on the lane, she was ready. Whoever it was wasn't going to see her in shorts and a skimpy top. She quickly slipped on a pair of nylon jogging pants and a T-shirt, then went to the window to see who was approaching. It was Ezra.

She opened the door after he rang the doorbell, "Hi, Ezra."

"Hello, Skye." She'd never noticed his eyes before, but he was standing so close to the door, she had to see them today. They weren't much to notice, really—not the bright blue of Dawdi's, or the dark brown of Bo's, or the green she shared with her birth mother. His eyes were just a pale, washed-out blue haze, and they didn't seem to say anything.

"I was going by on my way to town and thought I'd stop and see if you and Bo talked about those sheep," he said.

"We talked about it, yes, but we don't have the fence ready yet."

"Oh. Do you need help with the fence?"

Skye didn't know what to say. They could always use help. But she wasn't going to say yes to Ezra's offer without checking with Bo.

"I'll ask Bo," she answered. "We could let you know."

"Okay. Good. Well then, I guess I'll go."

"All right. See you, Ezra."

Ezra turned and walked down the porch steps toward his horse. The phone rang, and Skye went to answer it. It was Jake.

"Hey, what's happening in Kansas?" Jake's hyper voice enthused on the other end.

"Oh, not much. I just had my regular visit from the friendly-neighborhood-Amish-man. That's about as exciting as it gets around here."

"You really need to fly back here for a few days and get a life," Jake said. "Did you get those lyrics? What do you think?"

"I think I haven't decided," Skye answered just as the doorbell rang. She walked to the door and looked through the window. Ezra was standing on the porch.

"Uh, Jake, can I call you back?"

"Sure, babe—what's going on?"
"I'll tell you later."
"Okay, later."

Skye opened the door to see Ezra standing in the same position he'd been in just a few minutes earlier, only this time his pale eyes were pleading.

"Can I come in and talk to you, Skye?"

Something in his voice made her nod silently and close the door behind the mysterious bearded man.

SKYE
FOUR

SHE HAD NO IDEA what the man wanted with her or from her, and that scared Skye just a little. She'd never really thought that Ezra could be dangerous—strange, yes, but dangerous? Even when she noticed his eyes studying her, and when Bo half-joked about Ezra "having the hots" for her, she'd never taken it seriously. But now she'd invited him into her home, and she was alone. Was she crazy?

"Would you like to sit down?" she asked, watching the lanky man carefully.

"Yeah, that would be fine," he answered, and Skye heard the nervous tremor in his voice. Ezra took his straw hat off and set it on a chair near the door. He walked toward the booth in the corner of the kitchen and slid in.

"Nice idea," he said, rubbing his hands on the oak table in front of him.

"The booth? Thanks. Bo and I thought it would be neat to have one in the kitchen—kind of like being in a restaurant all the time—except for my cooking!" Skye laughed, hoping to lighten the tension in the room. "Would you like some tea?"

"Yes, that'd be good."

"Sugar?"

"Yes, please."

Skye poured tall glasses of sun tea for herself and Ezra and set them on the table. She got the sugar bowl and a spoon and placed them in front of him, then sat down across the table from him.

Ezra stirred his sugar for a long time, and Skye was beginning to wonder if she was going to have to open the conversation. About what, she didn't know.

Finally, he spoke, without looking up from his glass of tea.

"You and your real mother—are you getting along now?"

So, the same old topic. Skye stared at the man across the table from her. Why in the world was he so curious about her relationship with her mother? Maybe she'd finally find out.

"It's much better, yes. It won't always be easy—relationships never are. But forgiving her, and asking God to forgive me for holding the grudge against her—that's made a big, big difference." Skye paused. "Ezra, why do you keep asking about my mother?"

There, it was out.

Ezra took a drink of tea, then looked up into her eyes. "Because. . ." he began.

"First, I need to know that you won't be telling this to anyone," his faded blue eyes pleaded.

"I won't," Skye assured. "Except for Bo—I hope that's okay."

"As long as he keeps it to himself."

"He will."

Ezra cleared his throat and took another sip of tea.

"As you probably know, when Amish kids turn 16, they do a lot of wild and crazy things sometimes."

Skye nodded.

"One night, just a few months after I started running with the young folks, I went to a party. There were some English girls there—you know, not Amish. We all got drunk. I hadn't been drinking very long, so I didn't know how much I could have and still know what I was doing. I had too much."

Skye watched the Amish man's rough fingers playing with the glass of tea as he continued.

"To this day, I don't remember what happened that night. I do remember the others teasing me a lot the next day about the good time I'd had, but I had to take their word for it. I couldn't remember anything."

Ezra paused, and his eyes moved from his tea glass to the window, then back again to the glass. "Two months later I was at another party, and a girl came up to me. She looked familiar, and I knew she wasn't Amish. She pulled me aside and said we had to talk. Then she told me she was pregnant, and it was my baby."

Skye gasped quietly, then asked softly, "And how old were you?"

"Sixteen."

"Oh, my goodness."

"She said she didn't know what to do. She was thinking about having an abortion. I begged her please not to do that. She asked if I would support her if she kept it. What could I say? How could I support a girl and a baby? Where would I get the money, and how could I do it without my parents finding out?"

"What did you tell her?"

"Nothing, that evening. I said I needed time to think about it, and we agreed to meet again a week later. That was the worst week of my life."

"Did you talk to anybody about it?"

"No, nobody. Who could I tell? No, there wasn't anybody who could help me. I was 16, I'd fathered a child without knowing it, and now I was supposed to know what to do."

"What did you do?"

"I tried to talk her into giving it up for adoption. She finally agreed, and I thought that was the end of that horrible mistake. But I was reading the newspaper during the time I knew the baby was due, and I saw the birth announcement. The girl had decided to keep it after all. It was a little boy."

Skye sighed. Her heart went out to this man as he recalled his teenage trauma.

"I never heard from her again. But I can't forget it. Did she get married? Does my son have a father?"

"Do you know where they are?"

"No. She was from Vicksburg back then. I keep wondering if some day I'll see my boy and I won't know it's him. Or maybe I have already."

"Do you want to see him?"

Ezra drank the last of his tea and set the empty glass down on the table.

"I don't know."

"Does your wife know? Does anyone know?"

"I haven't told anyone."

"Do you think the boy's mother has told people?"

Ezra shrugged his shoulders.

"Sometimes the guilt almost kills me," he confessed. "I look at my other children, and I wonder if he looks like them. Someone will say something about 'my oldest son Cris,' and I'll think to myself 'no he's not—there's another one.' It's been very hard to live with. I feel like there is a part of me someplace that I need to know."

"I'm sure," Skye said quietly. "You know, if you want to find him, it shouldn't be too hard. I could help you."

Ezra got up from the booth and walked to the living room. For a long time he stood in front of the big south windows, his hands in his pockets, staring across the fields.

"I feel like a part of me will die if I don't ever see him, but if I do, and the community finds out, I will die of shame."

The words were quiet, but Skye could hear them in the stillness of the cedar log cabin. And she heard turmoil—the turmoil of a man fearing an emotional death no matter what he decided to do.

"I need to be going," Ezra said slowly, walking toward the kitchen.

"If I can do anything, let me know," Skye followed him with her eyes.

"I will," he said, picking up his hat from the chair. He set the hat on his head, and then, as if it gave him a small degree of confidence, looked Skye in the eye. "Thank you for listening."

"No problem. Anytime," she said, and she meant it. The Amish man would return to his wife and children, to his Amish community of tradition. But he had left a secret with her—a secret he had entrusted to the care of a "worldly woman." Perhaps that was why, Skye mused as she watched the horse and buggy clatter down the lane. Perhaps he trusted her with the sadness of his heart because he knew she'd been there too—in ways he feared his people would never understand.

***

"I had an Amish visitor this afternoon," Skye said later that day when Bo came home from his Harley shop in Vicksburg. She could hardly wait to tell him about Ezra, and he'd barely made it through the door when she made the announcement.

"Oh?" Bo said. He slipped his shoes off at the door and walked toward the table where the day's mail lay in a pile. He pulled the newspaper out of the stack and padded his way to the couch in his stocking feet. "And who might that have been?"

"A man," Skye said, deciding to tease Bo a little. She'd get him to pay attention to her.

"A man? Hmm.mm.mmm. Let me guess. Ezra stopped by to talk about sheep again," Bo said, opening up the newspaper and turning to the sports page.

"Half right."

Bo finally looked up. "Well, I don't know anyone else who talks to us about sheep, so it must have been Ezra."

"That's right. And he definitely didn't have sheep on his mind," Skye let the teasing drip out of her voice.

Bo was paying attention now. The paper went down as he looked at her and asked, "And just what did he have on his mind?"

"Oh, getting drunk, getting carried away with a woman—that kind of thing," Skye walked toward Bo and stood in front of him, grinning.

A mixture of confusion and disbelief saturated Bo's face, and Skye had to laugh out loud. She was being just a little bit mean, but after all, he was burying himself in the newspaper without even asking about her day.

"You're kidding, and it isn't funny," Bo said.

"No, I'm not, and yes it is," Skye bent down and wrapped her arms around his neck. "Actually, I'm not kidding, and it isn't funny," her voice grew serious.

"I'm listening," Bo said, the newspaper forgotten.

Skye sat down on the couch beside her husband. Then she told him Ezra's story, and when it was over, Bo let out a long, slow whistle.

"What a terrible position to be in," he said.

"For sure. I've been thinking about it a lot since he was here. I'm not sure why he confided in me. Maybe he thought I would understand. But it's not Ezra I identify with. It's his son—the child who's been denied the chance to know his father. You know what I mean?"

Bo nodded. "Maybe that's why he kept asking about your relationship with your mother. Maybe he wants to know if there's hope for him if he ever meets his son."

"I think you're right. But from what he said, and from what I know about the Amish, I can't quite imagine him doing it. "

"Why?"

"Because he would be the talk of the community."

"Would they shun him?"

Skye didn't answer right away, trying to remember what she knew about the traditions and rules of her grandparents' religion.

"We'd have to ask Dawdi, but I don't think so. Ezra's mistake happened before he was baptized and a member of the church, so he wouldn't have to confess and he wouldn't be shunned for what he did. It would be a different story if it happened after he'd joined."

"So the worst thing would be the gossip?"

"The gossip, and having his wife and family know. Can you imagine?"

"It'd be bad, I'm sure," Bo agreed. "It was strange enough to have everybody talking about our wedding because it was unusual."

"Exactly. And believe me, the gossip about our wedding was mild compared to what they'd say if word got out about Ezra. It'd take a long time for him to live it down."

"I'm betting he just needed to get it off his chest. He's told you, and he might keep talking about it, but he won't pursue finding the boy."

"I offered to help him if he really wants to do it."

"What did he say?"

"He said he felt like a part of him would die if he never saw his son, but if the community found out, he would die of shame. I'll never forget those words, or the look in his eyes when he said them."

SKYE

FIVE

THE MORNING AFTER Ezra's revelation to Skye, she got an e-mail message from her music producer in New York that made her put Ezra and his problems in the background. "Skye, we have to make some decisions about your next CD," Skye read the words on her monitor screen. "I think you should come to New York for a week so we can concentrate on this. Soon! Let me know. Jake."

Skye leaned back in her chair at the computer desk. He was right, of course. The wedding, getting settled into the house, her mother's visit—things other than her music career—had been taking up much of her time the last few months, and Jake was getting impatient. Used to be, she was addicted to her carreer—to the crowds, to the high she got when she was singing on stage, to the alcohol that flowed in the band and through her veins. In those days, Jake didn't have to worry about her commitment to her career—he just had to help keep her healthy. Now he had the opposite problem. Poor Jake, she laughed to herself.

Actually, there was nothing poor about Jake at all. Thanks to Skye's success in the music industry, his pocketbook was doing quite well. And Skye—well, she'd been able to pay for their log cabin without taking out a loan—a fact she knew still amazed people like her parents. Even Bo jokingly told people he married Skye for her money—a comment she always followed up by saying,

"Yes, honey, and I married you for your Harley's."

Skye smiled at the picture on her desk of Bo on his cycle. She pressed the button on her keyboard and scrolled down to the next e-mail message. It was from her mother Andrea. Nothing exciting—just a "Hi, how are you, here's what I've been doing" kind of note.

Skye rolled through the next group of messages—all from fans, some of them asking when her next CD would be out. Yes, yes, yes, she needed to get on with that. She'd write Jake back, set up a time, and buy the tickets.

A week later, Skye stood at 13th and Broadway in New York City, waiting for the light to change. She'd promised Bo she'd bring him "something very special and very New York," and she was on a mission. Jake had told her about a unique shop several blocks from the recording studio, so she was on her way to find the store and, hopefully, the perfect souvenir for her husband.

Her husband. It still sounded strange. After 35 years of being single, it still seemed hard to believe at times. It wasn't that she hadn't wanted to get married, or that she hadn't had her share of guys. But to actually be happily committed to one man—one man far away in Kansas—well, it wasn't exactly the Skye that her friends in New York remembered. And that was a fact they'd enjoyed rubbing in over the past few days.

Skye crossed the street with the many other people, each in their own world, each with an internal agenda. Hers was the store just a few doors down from the corner—Just Jim's, it was called.

She stepped into the shop, and her nose was immediately assaulted by the smell of incense. A thin young man with his blond hair cut very short and earrings in each ear stood behind the counter, watching her.

"Hi!" Skye said as she walked past the counter. And then she remembered. She wasn't in Kansas anymore. People in New York didn't greet strangers. She glanced back at him. He was still staring at her.

"I need to find something for my husband back in Kansas," she said, smiling. "I promised him it would be very 'New York.' Got any ideas?"

"What does he like?" the young man asked lightly. "Clothes, cologne, computers?"

"He owns a Harley shop, and he's thinking about buying sheep," Skye couldn't resist saying it, just to see the reaction.

The shopkeeper laughed—a high, pleasant laugh. "Harleys and sheep. Go figure. I'm sure you've heard this a million times before, but you look a lot like Skye. I love her music. I've got some posters in back from her last tour—why don't you buy one for your husband and say it's you. He could put it up in his Harley shop in—where did you say—Kansas?"

Skye could hardly keep from laughing out loud. This guy thought she looked like the famous rock star he admired. It hadn't occurred to him that she might be Skye. This would be fun.

"You know, that's a great idea," she said. "Do you really have one of those posters?"

"Those, and a lot of others. Would you like to see them?"

"Tell you what, I'll just take the one of Skye today," Skye said, pulling out her billfold. She slipped a credit card out and waited for him to return with the poster.

"See what I mean?" he unrolled the poster to its full length. It was the promotional poster from her tour with High Five—a long time ago, another life ago. Looking at the poster, she could almost see why he didn't recognize her. The woman staring at her was thinner, she was wearing tons of stage makeup, and she looked. . .angry? unhappy? wasted? Anyway, different—very different from the face Skye saw in the mirror these days.

"Yeah, I see what you mean," Skye smiled. "I think my husband will love it."

She handed him her credit card, and he slipped it through the machine. Then he gave her the receipt to sign, and she scrawled her name—Skye Martin. She handed him the receipt and smiled.

He stared at the receipt, then at her, and then the grin started. She could tell he was yelling inside—yelling for the sheer surprise of meeting her, and laughing for the silliness of selling a Skye poster to Skye herself. She knew he could hardly wait to tell his friends who came in his shop that day.

"Like I said, I thought you looked a lot like Skye," he giggled. "Why didn't you say something? Would you sign one of my posters?"

"You didn't tell me your name either," Skye teased. "Sure, I'll sign your poster."

"Jim. I own this shop," he said. "I'll be right back." Skye waited while her fan ran to get another poster, and while she waited, she wondered if she should get Bo something else from New York, or if this would be good enough.

※ ※ ※

Jake was right about it being easier for her to concentrate on her music in New York. Together they spent long hours in the studio, going through songs, deciding which ones to include in Skye's next release. Most of the CD seemed to be coming together, but she and Jake argued a whole morning over the lyrics he'd e-mailed her to look at. He liked them, and he thought they brought a variety to Skye's CD that would be good. She thought the words pushed some limits she didn't want to push.

But she didn't know how to say that to Jake. Skye? Not push the limits? She could hear it now. "What happened to you in Kansas? You get religion or something?"

Well, she didn't know about "getting religion." What she did know was that God was real to her in a new and exciting way, and her connection with God meant she approached life differently than she had before. It meant that some things that used to be exciting weren't anymore. And other things that would have been the ultimate in boredom a few years ago were now the desires of her heart.

She won the battle with Jake, of course. There was nothing he could do if she put her foot down and said she wouldn't sing the lyrics. It was, after all, her release. He stormed around the studio for a while, muttering, but he mellowed out. And when he said, "Next thing I know, you'll want to put a song on here that crosses over into Christian rock." Skye just smiled and said "How interesting that you should mention that. I've got this great songwriter back in Kansas. . ."

Skye laughed, letting Jake know she was only kidding. She just wanted to give him a hard time about his special songwriter. Actually, she did know a songwriter in Kansas that might try her hand at Christian lyrics one of these days. She lived in the middle of a Kansas pasture, was married to a man named Bo, and was right now feeling ready to leave the Big Apple to go back to the wide open spaces.

She called home that evening. Bo's deep bass voice answered the phone, and Skye loved it. She loved the sound of his voice, she loved knowing he was there, she loved having him belong to her. You've turned into a sissy romantic, she told herself. And she found herself loving that too.

"Hi, honey, how're you doing?" she asked.

"Just fine, considering I'm not used to banging around in a house by myself anymore," Bo answered. "It's a good thing your family is feeling sorry for me while you're gone—I've been eating at their places almost every night."

"Sounds like you're getting fed better than when I'm home," Skye laughed.

"I didn't say that."

"You didn't have to. That's okay. Being around my Amish family should keep you out of trouble."

"Yeah. I did go out with the guys one night in Vicksburg."

"Bo. . ."

"Don't worry. I didn't do anything you wouldn't do."

"In which part of my life?" Skye tried not to sound worried or overly protective.

Bo laughed his slow low laugh. "You don't need to worry about me, Skye. You're the one in New York City with your friends—I should be asking you what you've been doing."

"Working hard, and missing you."

"I like that."

"It's true."

"Do you have the next CD planned out?"

"Yes, I had to fight with Jake over that one song—you know, the lyrics I showed you. I didn't tell him this, but I couldn't imagine facing people in Wellsford if I'd sung that song. Truth is, I couldn't face myself."

"I know what you mean."

"So, anything exciting happening there?"

"I finished the sheep fence. So, next time I see Ezra, I'll ask him if he has some sheep to sell."

"Has Ezra stopped in?"

"I guess that depends on what you mean by 'stopped in.' I haven't seen him. But your family was telling me that they've seen him either turning into our lane or coming out of it almost every day. They know you're gone, so they can't figure out what he's doing here. Some other people have noticed, and they're starting to talk. They know I'm gone during the day, and you're often at home. Joe Miller, the guy down the road, jokingly asked me yesterday if my wife was teaching Ezra Yoder how to sing, since he seemed to be over here a lot. "

"Oh, no."

"Oh, yes. So you have something to look forward to when you come home."

"I have a lot to look forward to, Bo. And believe me, it has nothing to do with Ezra and gossipy people."

"Just thought I'd warn you, in case the newspaper reporters meet you at the airport."

"You *are* kidding."

"Yeah, I'm kidding. On the other hand, you never know about the media. After all, you are a star."

"Well this *star* is going to finish up here as soon as possible and come home to you, because *you* are what she's looking forward to."

"Don't forget my souvenir."

"I've got it already—you won't believe what I found for you."

"I have a surprise for you too."

"Really? Oh, Bo, what is it? Give me a hint!"

"No hints. Just hurry home."

"I will, honey, I will."

SKYE
SIX

Skye stepped out of the commuter plane at the Vicksburg airport and into the August oven of Kansas. It was hot, but so was New York. Here at least there was a wind blowing the hot air around, and there was space for a person to breathe. A week of the crowded conditions of the city, and she was ready to come home. Home to the country, to Bo, and to the surprise he had waiting for her. She felt like a little kid, wondering what her daddy brought home from his business trip for her.

Thirty minutes later, Skye parked her car beside Bo's Harley shop and stepped out. She walked in and spotted him right away—he was in the back, tinkering on a bike. He'd heard the bell ring when the door opened, and was walking toward her, a big smile on his face.

"Welcome back, honey," he said in that voice she never tired of hearing. She walked into his arms, smelling his cologne as he drew her to him. He held her, then kissed her gently.

"It's good to be home," she said.

"Were your flights okay?" he asked, backing away a bit, his eyes searching hers.

"Fine, no problems. And what about here? Anything new and exciting?"

"New and exciting? Might be. We'll have to see what you think."

"What? What are you talking about, Bo?"

"Where's my souvenir?" he asked, ignoring her question.

"And where's my surprise?"

"At home."

"Well, that's where you'll get your souvenir too."

"Oh." Bo looked at his watch. "Sure wish it were time to close."

"Maybe you could close early today—please?"

"I don't know. . ."

"Just this once. . .or else I'm going home alone to start looking for my surprise. And I will look until I find it," Skye teased.

Bo looked at his watch again, then at Skye. "You know I might miss a big sale."

"Nobody's going to come buy a bike today—it's too hot."

"You don't make a lot of sense, my dear wife, but I can't let you go home alone, and I can't make you sit here and wait for me. So I guess I'll have to take my chances," Bo said, reaching for the chain of keys looped to his pants. "I'll lock up, and we'll go."

🐑 🐑 🐑

Skye followed Bo on his cycle as they drove the hour it took to reach their home. They turned into the lane leading through the pasture to their cabin, nestled away from the road. Skye stopped the car, stepped out, and heard it immediately. Barking.

She ran after Bo, who'd walked behind the house as soon as he got off his cycle. Skye turned the corner into their backyard, and there they were—Bo and a squirmy black-and-white puppy. Both were grinning from ear to ear.

"Oh, Bo! What in the world? Where did you get him?" Skye crouched down on the ground beside her husband and wriggly puppy.

"It's your surprise. I figured a farm with sheep needs a sheep dog, so here he is. Do you like him?"

"He's adorable! What kind is he?" Skye asked, wrapping her

arms around the canine bundle.

"Border collie. The kind that herds sheep."

"Where did you get him?'

"Guess."

"Guess? How would I know?"

"Ezra."

"Ezra! Is that why he was always coming over? He wanted to give us a puppy?"

"Half right. He wanted to *sell* us a puppy."

"Oh! How much did you cost, you silly little guy?" Skye nuzzled the soft black-and-white body, earning a face wash in return.

The puppy didn't answer her question, and neither did Bo. When Skye finally looked up at Bo, he smiled and said, "More than I've ever paid for a dog before."

"Have you ever *bought* a dog before?"

"No."

"Well then."

"Ezra said he comes with herding instincts built into him, but we'll need to train him too. I think Ezra was hoping he could help you train the dog," Bo said, and Skye heard the teasing in his voice.

"Oh, I can hardly wait," Skye decided to play along with Bo's insinuation. "We'll go over to Ezra's tomorrow and get started."

"Not so fast, young lady," Bo laughed. "For one thing, he's just six weeks old. You have to wait until he's grown up. And for another thing, Ezra's not interested in you—it's his son he's after."

"Oh, yeah, you're right," Skye said. "So, does this little critter have a name?"

"Nope, I was going to let you do that."

Skye studied the border collie puppy as he frisked around the yard, smelling, running, bouncing. Should his name have something to do with his coloring? His job in life? His personality?

Maybe she'd need a couple of days to think about it.

"What's his mother's name?"

"I don't know. You'd have to ask Ezra."

When it came to her a few minutes later, Skye wondered if she should even say what she was thinking. She would. Bo had said she could name the puppy.

"Zebediah."

"Zebediah?" Bo's raised eyebrows and "I don't believe it" face were what she'd expected.

"Yep. He has the colors of a zebra, so that made me think of Zeb. And coming from Ezra, he should have something that sounds like an Old Testament name. Zebediah. We'll call him Zeb."

Bo laughed. "All I can say is, I'm glad we don't have children. I can't imagine what kind of names their mother would come up with for them."

Skye gave him her "give me a break" look and reached for the puppy, who'd settled down next to where Bo sat on the ground. "Come here, little Zeb," she said, holding his face between her hands and looking into the bright dark eyes. "When you're naughty you will be *Zebediah!* Got that, my little buddy boy?"

The puppy squirmed out of her hands and rolled onto his back. Bo reached over and scratched Zebediah's tummy. Skye smiled. She loved her surprise.

※ ※ ※

Bo had suggested they go to Wellsford for supper, and it sounded good to Skye. She decided to take his souvenir along—it'd be a great story to tell him over the meal. Plus, she knew many of the waitresses who worked in the Deutschland Restaurant. They'd get a kick out of the story and the poster too.

They sat side-by-side in one of the booths and ordered what they always ordered—Bo, a cheeseburger with onion rings, and Skye, a chef salad. Skye had carried a large paper tube in with her, and she handed it to him. "Here's your present," she grinned. "I hope you like it, because I spent a lot of money for it."

Bo looked puzzled as he popped off the cap on one end and slid the poster out. He looked even more confused when he unrolled the poster and came face to face with the Skye of a few years earlier.

"Let me guess. You forgot to get me something and you pulled this out of Jake's studio right before you left for the airport," he said, half-grinning.

"No, no, no!" Skye protested. "Listen!"

She proceeded to tell him the story of how she found the poster and Jim, who didn't know she was Skye.

"That is crazy," Bo agreed. "Yeah, that makes this poster worth more, and you're right, it is very 'New York.'"

"Look at the back side—it'll make the poster worth more to you too," Skye said, her voice flirting.

Bo turned the large sheet over and began to read the note in Skye's handwriting. He started to smile, to beam, and then he whistled under his breath. "Yes," he said. "I like this. I like this very much. Nice poster. Very, very nice."

Skye laughed out loud. Men. Give them a coupon for a hot romantic evening together, and they'll be happier than if you spent a lot of money. What a deal.

❧ ❧ ❧

They stopped to see Jonas and Sue Ann on the way home that evening—Bo had promised they'd do that soon after Skye returned. The grandparents were always thrilled to see members of their family, and they had worried about Skye the week she was gone. Skye knew it was a good thing they didn't know the details of her years spent doing concert tours—they would have been worried sick. Now that she lived nearby, they kept close tabs on her. Sometimes she wondered if they remembered she was in her mid-30's—an adult who could take care of herself. But then she realized she would always be their granddaughter, and she remembered the times when their years of wisdom were exactly what she needed. Like the evening she spent with Jonas in the pasture, forgiving her mother, giving herself permission to start over.

Jonas and Sue Ann were sitting on their porch that hot evening when Bo and Skye turned onto the lane. They jumped off the cycle and walked toward the old Amish couple. Jonas's newspaper rested in his lap, and Sue Ann's knitting in hers. Skye gave them each a hug, then sat down on a chair next to her grandmother.

"How was New York?" Sue Ann looked at Skye, her dark eyes bright in her wrinkled tan face. "Was it hot there too?"

"Yes, very. And lots of people. It was okay to be there to get my work done, but I'm glad to be back home."

"We're glad you're back too," Jonas said. "I just wish you would have found some cool weather and brought it with you," he wiped his forehead with his hand.

"I'm sorry, but I don't see how you can sleep in that house without air-conditioning or fans," Skye said. "I don't think I could do it."

"Ach, it's all what you get used to," Jonas said. "You used to do it all the time when you and Angela came to visit us during the summer."

"You're right, we did," Skye agreed. "Some things are harder to do when you're older," she continued, and then realized what she'd said. "I guess that excuse doesn't hold much water when I say it to you, does it?"

Sue Ann, Jonas, and Bo laughed, and Skye joined them.

"Did Bo tell you what he got for me—for us?" she changed the subject.

"You mean the puppy? Yes, Bo showed him to us," Jonas answered. "Ezra was here trying to get Emma and Caleb to take one too."

"Did they?"

"No. They didn't want to spend money on a dog when there are always free ones to be had."

"But Zebediah is a very special dog, and he's going to help us with our sheep."

"Zebediah?" Sue Ann looked at Skye and her eyes were twinkling.

"That's what I said," Bo pitched in.

"We'll call him Zeb," Skye said, half-defensively.

"I told her it's a good thing we don't have kids for her to name," Bo teased, and Jonas and Sue Ann chuckled.

"I'll tell Ezra he should have named the dog before he sold him to you," Jonas joked. "Something like Shep."

"Shep, Zeb, what's the difference?" Skye wanted to know.

"It's okay, Skye," Sue Ann came to her defense. "It's not such a bad name—religious names kind of run in the family. I know a man who once had a horse named Preacher." She turned to smile at her husband, and Jonas smiled back.

SKYE

SEVEN

Skye let herself sleep in the day after her return to Kansas. She had worked hard in New York, and didn't feel bad at all about going back to sleep after Bo said good-bye that morning. She relaxed in the luxury of their king-sized waterbed and drifted away.

The clop-clop-clop of a horse's hooves and the rattle of buggy wheels coming down the lane woke her with a start. Skye looked at the clock—9:00. And she was still in bed. Now she remembered her grandfather saying he might stop in on his way to Wellsford in the morning. He hadn't said what time, but this was probably the middle of the morning for him.

Skye rolled out of the waterbed and slipped on a pair of jean shorts and T-shirt. She ran a brush through her hair, made a face at herself in the mirror, and called it good enough. Her grandfather wouldn't care how she looked, she consoled herself.

The doorbell rang and she went to open the door.

There stood Ezra.

"Oh! Good morning," Skye managed.

"Morning. Thought I'd stop and see how you're gettin' along with the puppy," Ezra's eyes shifted from Skye's face to the yard. "You've still got him, don't ya?"

"Sure! Sure! He's a sweetheart. He should be in the back

yard." Skye walked across the porch, down the steps, and around the house, with Ezra following a few steps behind.

Zebediah was sitting in the small pen Bo had built for him, his ears and eyes alert to the sounds coming from a part of the yard he couldn't see. The minute he saw Skye and Ezra, he started barking and jumping against the fence.

"He's a frisky one," Ezra commented, walking toward the pen. "Best one in the litter. Smart. I could tell that from the start."

Skye opened the gate and Zeb was out, a black-and-white bundle of wagging tail, bright eyes, and long red tongue. Apparently he couldn't decide who to greet first or with the most enthusiasm, so he ran between Skye and Ezra, showering both with puppy-love.

Skye laughed as she bent down to play with Zeb. Ezra crouched down beside her and Zeb. "He'll make a good sheep dog for ya," he said. "Only thing you're missing now are the sheep."

"You're right. Do you have some to sell?"

"I might. You and Bo come over sometime and look."

"We'll do that."

Skye stood up and looked down at Ezra, who was still playing with Zeb. Was this really why he was here? Or did he want to talk about his son? And if he did, how long would it take him to get around to it?

"So, have you thought more about looking for your son?" Skye asked. Between her and her twin sister, Angela, she'd always been the more forthright, doesn't-beat-around-the-bush type. Sometimes that characteristic got her in hot water. Sometimes, in her opinion, it just cut out a lot of the garbage people said while they were waiting to say what they really wanted to communicate.

Ezra stood up slowly, but his eyes didn't leave the puppy.

"Yeah, I have," he paused. "If you would, I'd like for you to see what you can find."

"Have you told Lizzie?" Skye asked. She knew it was really none of her business what Ezra told his wife. But she also knew that taking steps to find Ezra's first son would set in motion a chain of events that could be healthy, hurtful, or both for Ezra and his family.

"No. I don't see any point right now. Not until we find him, anyway."

"What's the woman's name—the mother of your boy?"

"It was Verdene. Verdene Johnson. But she could be married now."

"Did you sign papers releasing your rights to the baby?"

"No. I thought I would do that after it was born, when it was adopted. But then Verdene kept him."

"So, legally you are still responsible for him," Skye said. "She never came after you for child support?"

Ezra shook his head.

"Do you realize she still could?"

Ezra nodded his head slowly.

"Especially if you get in touch with him—and Verdene. I'd think they'd go after you for all these years of failing to pay child support."

Ezra's faded blue eyes looked into Skye's. "How much could that be?"

"A lot," Skye said, her voice heavy. *A lot more than you have, Ezra*, she thought to herself.

"Do you think she would do that?"

"I don't know her at all. Do *you* think she would?"

Ezra scuffed at the ground with his worn work shoe. "I don't know her at all either."

She's the mother of your son, Skye thought, *and you know less about her than you do about this puppy you raised.*

The words had no more passed through her mind than a bolt of guilt and realization followed them. Who was she to talk? Skye

Martin, the rock star who had partied, entertained men, and thumbed her nose at the values and standards she'd grown up with in her Mennonite home. Skye Martin could be in the same position Ezra Yoder was in today—knowing nothing about the other person who shared responsibility for the creation of a baby. It hadn't happened to her, but it could have.

Ezra had sought her out because he hoped she'd understand. He had come to her because her biological mother had left her behind as a baby, and because now she was reunited with her mother. But whether he knew it or not, Skye understood Ezra's position on another level entirely. She'd been there. Done that. She didn't have a child somewhere to point the finger of guilt at her, but she'd made the same mistakes.

Fortunately, she had confessed and received God's forgiveness. She remembered her past, but it no longer bound her in guilty knots. She wondered if Ezra had gone through a forgiveness experience. Maybe she'd ask him someday.

"I still want you to find out what you can," Ezra said, bringing Skye back from her internal journey. "How will you do that?"

"It shouldn't be hard, but I may need your signature saying that you, the father, are initiating the search. I'll have to get the right paperwork and we'll go from there."

"Okay." Ezra sounded relieved and scared.

"You can still back out any time, until we actually make contact."

"I know."

***

He was back the next day. This time Skye was ready for Ezra. Thanks to the wealth of information on the Internet, she'd downloaded the form he'd need to sign to authorize the search for his son. She handed it and a pen to him, wondering if he'd back out now. He took a long time to read the words on the form, then slowly scrawled his name and the date at the bottom of the page.

※ ※ ※

That evening, it was Skye and Bo's turn to visit Ezra. He lived just a mile away, on a small dairy farm.

If she could paint, it would be the kind of scene she'd love to paint, Skye thought as they neared the farm. "Kansas Amish Family Farm," she'd call it. The yard hummed with life—chickens scratching in the garden, children playing on a little red wagon, puppies running everywhere, sheep grazing between the buildings, Holstein cows making their way out to the pasture after being milked. Bright flowers smiled from their spots in front of the white picket fence. Behind the fence, rows of laundry hung on the wash lines, testifying to the conservative traditions of the family living there—dark homemade barn-door pants, dark and pastel simple dresses, light-colored men's and boys' shirts. And normal underwear. Skye giggled.

"What's so funny?" Bo asked from in front of her on the Harley.

"I saw their laundry hanging out, and I remembered some of the questions tourists ask in Gary County about the Amish. One of them is 'Do the Amish wear homemade underwear?'"

Bo laughed. "Looks like regular underwear to me."

They roared into the yard, instantly impacting the serene scene. Puppies scampered for cover, children scurried for the house to watch from the safety of the door, and the sheep ran from the noisy Harley. Bo turned the bike off, and he and Skye slid off. Skye saw Lizzie approaching them from the garden.

"Hello," the Amish woman greeted them.

"Hi, Lizzie," Skye answered. "Ezra told us to stop by sometime and take a look at the sheep. I guess he wants to sell a few, and now that we have a sheep dog, we probably should have some sheep."

Lizzie smiled. "Yes, you got the best puppy in the litter, I think. As you can see, we still have a few left. Don't you want another one?"

"Oh, no, one's enough," Bo answered quickly.

"Cris!" Lizzie called, turning toward the house. "Cris! Come here!"

Skye watched as the ten-year-old boy walked barefoot toward them, his left leg in a light plastic cast.

"How's the leg, Cris?" Bo asked.

"It's okay, but the cast is so hot," Cris answered.

"It's been hard for him because he's such an active boy," Lizzie added. "But we're glad it wasn't worse."

"Sure scared me when I saw him fall and that wagon run over him," Bo remembered. "You're right, it could have been worse."

"Cris, show Bo and Skye the sheep. Dad's gonna sell them some." Lizzie turned toward Bo and Skye. "Do you want old ewes or ewe lambs?"

Skye glanced at Bo. He shrugged. She looked back at Lizzie. "You tell us. What do we want—old ewes or ewe lambs?"

Lizzie and Cris both laughed. The other four little barefoot Yoders had gotten brave enough to join their mother and brother, and they tittered from behind Lizzie's skirts.

"They think we don't know anything about sheep," Skye pretended to be offended.

"Do we?" Bo asked. "Cris, show us those old ee-yews or ee-yew lambs."

"Bo, it's ewes. It sounds just like 'use.' Ewes," Skye corrected.

"A's, e's, i's, o's, u's—why is it spelled with two e's if it sounds like u's?" Bo chuckled. "Cris, you know the anwer to that one?"

Cris shook his head and began walking toward the corner of the yard where the sheep had gathered after Bo's cycle scared them. They eyed the newcomers warily.

"We have 20 ewes—females—that have had lambs before,"

Cris explained. "And we have 15 ewe lambs—girls."

"How can you tell the difference?" Skye wondered, staring at the sea of wooly white faces gazing back at her.

"The lambs are smaller and they look younger."

"I could have told you that," Bo kidded. "The *ewes* are definitely bigger."

"Well, it's hard to see when they're all jammed together."

"Do you want me to chase them out of the corner?" Cris asked.

"No, that's okay," Skye assured. "Are the ewes bred?"

"They should be—Dad had the buck in with them."

"When would they have lambs?"

"I don't know. You'll have to ask Dad."

"What about the young ewes?" Bo asked.

"I'm not sure. You'll have to ask Dad."

"I like that one with the brown markings on her face," Skye pointed.

"She was a bottle lamb," Cris said. "She's pretty tame."

"Where *is* your dad?" Bo asked.

"Working in the field," Cris said. "Where I should be, except for this stupid cast."

"Does it keep you from riding cycle?" Bo asked, a twinkle in his eye.

"I don't have…" Cris began, and then a big grin spread across his face.

"No," he answered.

"Then go ask your mom if it's okay."

Skye couldn't believe how fast a ten-year-old boy could run with one strong leg and one in a cast.

SKYE

EIGHT

A WEEK AFTER THEIR VISIT to Ezra's farm, Bo and Skye were sheep owners. Five ewes that had belonged to Ezra were now a part of the picture in Bo and Skye's ten-acre plot. The small herd grazed during the cooler morning and evening hours, and spent much of the daytime contentedly chewing their cuds under the shade trees. Zebediah knew he was supposed to do something with them, but at this point his immaturity far outweighed his wisdom, and he just wanted to bark and make them run.

Skye decided to name the sheep. Bo chuckled, and then tried to tell her that these sheep were livestock, not pets. Skye said she didn't know what that had to do with giving them names, and proceeded anyway. The tame one with the brown markings on her face was Molly. Misty had finer wool than the others, and Maggie was a Suffolk with a black face and legs. Muffin was another brown face that wasn't as tame, and Mud had her name when they got her. "We found her in the mud when she was just born, and we had to rescue her and give her a bottle until she was strong enough to nurse," Cris had explained. Mud was a Suffolk too, so her black body parts matched her name.

"Looks to me like Ezra sold us his misfits," Bo said that evening as he and Skye stood by the fence, watching their livestock investment.

"What do you mean? They all look fine to me."

"Didn't you notice? His herd was almost all white faces—I think he called them Dorsets. We got the ones that didn't fit in."

"Well, that's fine with me, because now I can tell them apart," Skye said, running through the ewes' names and characteristics in her mind. "I like it better if they don't all look alike."

"As long as they keep the grass down and give us healthy lambs, I really don't care what color they are," Bo said, reaching down to pet Zebediah, who was on a leash between them. Zeb responded with eager, upturned eyes. "You wanna go play some frisbee, Zeb?"

Of course he did. Bo got a frisbee from the house and threw it for Zeb, who had caught on quite naturally to the idea of catching the saucer and returning it to the thrower. Skye said she was going inside to make some phone calls.

One of the calls she needed to return was from a woman in Vicksburg. Mary Lou Somebody. She didn't know the woman, or why she was calling. Probably the media, Skye surmised. But the woman hadn't mentioned being with a newspaper, magazine, or television station when she left the message on the answering machine. Just said "It's somewhat urgent, and I'd really appreciate your returning my call."

Skye dialed the number, and on the third ring, a child's voice answered the phone.

"Hello, this is Travis John Wenger," the voice said.

"Hi Travis, is your mommy there?"

"Yeah, Mom—eeee!" the voice yelled into Skye's ear. "Tel-e-phone!"

Moments later a woman's voice said hello.

"Mary Lou, this is Skye Martin returning you call."

"Oh! Thank you for calling back. I really appreciate it." The voice sounded young and pleasant, and Skye wondered again what Mary Lou wanted from her.

"No problem," Skye said. "You have quite the little answering person there."

"Yes, Travis is just starting to answer the phone, and he runs for it when it rings," Mary Lou said. "Skye, I know this might be a long shot, but I'm calling to see if you would consider singing at a picnic our company is having. We had our entertainment all lined up and they backed out at the last minute. Someone suggested I call you. I know we can't begin to afford what you normally get for a concert, and this is really late notice, but, well, we thought it couldn't hurt to ask."

"When is this picnic?"

"This Saturday."

"You mean like day after tomorrow?"

"I know it's late notice. We had no idea our group would cancel out."

"Where and how long?"

"In Pioneer Park. However long you want to sing—maybe an hour?"

Skye knew the money would be incidental. She also knew that she didn't want to start doing a lot of small local concerts. Saying yes to one could certainly lead to more. She should just say no and leave it at that. But the poor woman. . .

"I don't have a band here, so I'd have to sing with a soundtrack," she heard herself saying.

"That'd be fine. Just fine!"

"How many people?"

"Oh, we usually have about 500 at our picnic, including kids."

Skye wasn't sure why, but she heard herself saying yes. And she heard Mary Lou say thank-you—it was the voice of an adult woman who could hardly keep from screaming like an excited kid.

꧁ ꧁ ꧁

The next day, Friday, Skye was planning her concert and

dubbing soundtracks onto one cassette when Ezra showed up. He wanted to see how the sheep were doing, and yes, he wanted to know if Skye had come up with anything on his son. She admitted that she hadn't, but she hadn't put a lot of time into it either. It'd only been a week since Ezra had signed the papers authorizing the search. Skye had been busy catching up on her mail and e-mail since returning from New York, and learning a song for the new CD. She'd made a few phone calls and done a little bit of research on the Internet, but that was as far as she'd gotten. She promised to keep at it. But it wouldn't happen overnight. She would let him know as soon as she came across something, she assured Ezra.

What she wanted to say was "Don't call me—I'll call you." But she couldn't bring herself to tell Ezra those words. As much as she needed some time and space to get her work done, and as much as Ezra's visits interrupted her day, she couldn't tell him not to come over. There might have been a time in her life when she wouldn't mind being that rude, but not anymore. It seemed very uncharacteristic of Jesus to say "I don't have time for you," and if she was claiming to follow him, she'd have to follow him in attitude too. It wasn't always easy.

Skye decided to call her parents in Pennsylvania that evening. She hadn't talked to them since Ezra's "assignment" for her. It was time to catch up with Ken and Becca.

Becca's lively voice answered the phone, and Skye smiled as she greeted her mother. There were many things about the woman who'd raised her—the woman she'd called "mommy"—that Skye saw in herself. People who didn't know that Skye and her twin sister, Angela, were adopted could easily assume Skye inherited Becca's independence and nonconformity. And by the same token, Angela had carried a sensitive, peaceful spirit a lot like Ken's.

"So what's happening in Touristland?" Skye asked her mother, knowing this was the time of year that families were taking vacations to go "Amish watching," as Becca jokingly called it.

"Oh, it's busy as usual," Becca answered. "I've had to hire a couple of extra girls to give rides, and add some horses too. It's been a good summer so far."

Skye remembered her summers growing up in Gary County. Her mother owned a buggy rides business, and she hired young women, many of them Amish, to give the rides. Skye hadn't ever given rides—she wasn't that confident of herself with the horse and a buggy full of tourists, but she'd spent many hours cleaning out the stable, feeding, and caring for the horses. Her mother still owned the thriving business.

"Are you and Dad going to come visit us this fall, when things slow down?" Skye asked.

"We'd like to. And how about you? When will you come up to see us?"

"I don't know, now that we have *animals to take care of*, it'll be hard to get away."

"Oh?"

"Yeah, we bought a herd of sheep from an Amish guy, and Bo got us a border collie puppy that's supposed to work with the sheep."

"A herd? How big is a herd?"

"Five," Skye giggled.

"Ken, they have a *herd* of five sheep," Becca told her husband. "And a dog! Our daughter is now a full-time farmer!"

Skye heard her parents laughing on the other end of the line. Her father had picked up the extension and was now in the conversation as well.

"Do I hear some *schput* being made about me?" Skye pretended to be offended.

"Now, Skye, we wouldn't make fun of your agricultural endeavors," her father said. "Tell me, do you still have time for your music?"

"Dad! See if I ever tell you two anything again!"

"Sorry, honey. You know we're kidding," Ken said. "Seriously, when is your next CD going to be out? The one you worked on in New York?"

Skye and her parents talked about her CD, and Skye told them about the concert she had agreed to give the next day. Then she told them about Ezra's revelation, and his request that she try to find his son.

"I hope you know what you're getting into," Becca warned.

"What do you mean?"

"You're opening a can of worms. You've got Ezra, his wife and family, his son that he's never seen, the mother of his son, and probably a husband and other kids—all of those people who would be dealing with the feelings this is going to bring up. Not to mention the community talk that's going to go around. Does Ezra have any idea what he's in for?"

"I don't think so. But who am I to tell him he can't find his son?"

"You can't," Ken said. "But be prepared for him to lean on you a lot through this process, because you and Bo will probably be the only people he can talk to about what's happening."

"I know, I know. If you would have told me two years ago that I'd be living in Kansas, helping an Amish man find his son, I would have said you're crazy. I guess God does some surprising things sometimes."

"You can say that again," Ken agreed. "Don't we all know."

And they certainly did. The unusual, inexplicable events that brought Skye and her sister into the lives of Ken and Becca had always been called a miracle. It was a story Ken never tired of telling, and Skye knew it still brought tears to his eyes 35 years after it happened.

"Keep us posted on what happens with your search," Becca said. "We'll be praying."

"Thanks, Mom and Dad, I will."

They talked for a few more minutes, and then said good-bye. Skye breathed a prayer of thanksgiving for her parents, and asked God for an equally positive outcome for Ezra and his son.

❧ ❧ ❧

The concert the next evening at Pioneer Park wasn't a new experience for Skye, but it certainly had been a long time. When she and Angela were young, they'd been popular entertainers in Gary County. "The Martin Twins" sang for a wide variety of groups and occasions, and outdoor concerts had been a part of that.

But after their high school graduation, the twins' lives took different paths. Skye accepted an invitation from Jake Jordan to audition for a band in New York, and her career had grown from there. Any outdoor concerts she might have done wouldn't have been exactly called "family entertainment."

But now her life had changed, and she found it refreshing to be singing to an audience of families. If an outside concert on an August evening could be called "refreshing," that is.

She sang for an hour, and she could tell from the attentiveness and lack of movement in the crowd that she could have gone longer. But she was running out of songs that she felt good about singing in front of this group, and it was time to wrap it up. Skye pulled a faded red bandanna out of the back pocket of her jeans and spoke softly into the mic.

"I want to tell you a story," Skye paused, fingering the bandanna. "I am a twin. My sister Angela and I grew up in Pennsylvania, but we came to Wellsford every summer to stay with our grandparents, who are Amish. One summer our uncle gave us each a harmonica. We were seven years old. Angela learned to play hers right away, but I didn't want to take time to practice. The evening before we were going to fly back home to Pennsylvania, Angela played her harmonica for our Amish relatives, and she was very good. I got mad. I stole her harmonica and I threw it in the outhouse." Skye paused. "I guess you could say I was a little stinker, and that was a very nasty thing to do."

The crowd chuckled, and then Skye continued. "My wise and wonderful grandfather talked to me that evening, and helped me to understand why I'd done that, and how unfair it was to Angela. I cried a lot, and he gave me this bandanna. He said I should keep it with me for other times when I would need to cry.

"As many of you know, I took this bandanna with me on the road when I was doing concert tours. And as you also know, I needed it desperately when Angela died a year ago. Angela was good and caring when I was bad and self-centered. She gave herself to others while I was satisfying myself. In the end, she gave her life for me." Skye paused. The audience seemed to be holding its breath.

"She gave her life for me, just like Christ did for humanity. I am here with you today because I know both to be true with all my heart."

The beginning chords of a song slipped out of the speakers and over the crowd—the song Skye wrote after Angela's death. "Angela, this one's for you," Skye said softly, and then began to sing.

Even though we were twins and very small
we were never like each other at all.
You wanted to stay close to home,
and I had a passion to roam and roam.
Somehow your world was tidy and safe,
but my path took me to another kind of place.
You were a caterpillar crawling on the ground,
the blue Skye of my name my butterfly wings found.

Sisters, our paths have parted now,
sisters, how can I go on—I'll have to find out how
to keep travelin' this road,

*when you have left me and taken a part of my soul,
oh Angela, Angela...*

*Older, you had babies and were a farmer's wife,
I became a rock star and traveled the skies.
You never left the boundaries of our childhood,
living a secure life I never thought I could...
But even though you've left the earth, you're still not too far
to know my music is longing to reach your heart.
It's never too late to share our lives,
don't leave me now to fly alone in the sky...*

Skye felt emotions rolling like waves in her as she sang the chorus again, knowing that she had to hold herself together for the remainder of the song.

*Angela, when you were on earth with me,
you finally made me see,
it was okay to let down and trust,
you gave me so much that you died from your love.*

*I never was as sure about God as you,
no matter how far I searched I never quite knew,
if God was listening to all my songs of life,
or if they touched his heart and if he cried?
But this one's for you, Angela, I know you're up above,
tell heaven I'm singing you a song of my love,
And until I get there to share that home,
always know you have a part of my soul.*

*Sisters, our paths have parted now,
sisters, I will go on—I do know how...
I can keep travelin' this road,*

*even though you've left and taken a part of my soul,
oh Angela, Angela.**

The last notes faded from the speakers as Skye stood on the stage, her head bowed, her face wet. She wiped her eyes with the bandanna, then looked up and said, "Thank-you. May God be with you."

Skye left the stage. The applause followed her footsteps and begged her to return, but she had no more to give.

---

* *"Sisters," (Angela's Song)* © *1997 by Laurie L. Oswald*

SKYE

NINE

THE STAGE IN PIONEER PARK didn't provide a private place for Skye to retreat to after her concert, but Mary Lou had arranged for an RV for her to use. Skye was sitting in the RV with Bo and Mary Lou, enjoying a glass of iced tea and the air-conditioning, when there was a knock on the door. Mary Lou went to the door and opened it.

"Um, I know this might not be possible, but I was wondering. . .I was wondering if I could possibly talk to Skye for a minute?" Skye heard a female voice saying to Mary Lou.

"I can ask her," Mary Lou responded. "What's your name?"

"Verdene Johnson."

Skye's heart flipped. Verdene Johnson?!!

Skye stood up and walked toward the door. "Come on in, Verdene."

A woman in her mid-30's stepped up into the RV. She smiled hesitantly at Skye.

"I don't want to bother you, but. . .if I could have just a few minutes with you. . .alone?" Verdene asked, her eyes moving from Skye to Bo to Mary Lou.

"Sure, we can do that," Skye agreed.

Bo and Mary Lou left, and Skye turned to Verdene.

"Would you like some tea?"

"Yes, please, that would be great."

"I don't know why I'm bothering you with this," Verdene sat down at the small table. She seemed to be in a hurry to say what she'd come to say. "When I heard you talk about your Amish relatives. . .well. . .as much as I didn't want to come talk to you, something told me I had to. I had to come talk about a secret I've kept for over seventeen years."

Skye knew what was coming. But of course Verdene had no idea that she knew. What an incredible stroke of luck, Skye thought. And then she caught herself. Luck? No way. Divine intervention. Plain and simple.

"I'm listening."

"When I was a teenager, a bunch of us girls would often go party with the Amish kids in Wellsford," Verdene began. "We had a great time with them, but. . .but I ended up getting pregnant. I didn't even really know the guy. I had a baby boy, and even though I'd decided to give it up for adoption, I couldn't. I kept him. He's seventeen now. He's a good kid, but he's been bugging me about who his father is. I haven't ever told him because I don't want to embarrass his father—you know, the Amish—they'd probably never let him live it down. So I just tell Jason that his father disappeared from my life when I was pregnant with him, and I don't know where he is. The older he gets, the less willing he is to take that answer."

Verdene spilled her story quickly, as if she'd made a deal with herself that she could leave as soon as she'd told Skye. She continued, her words tumbling after each other.

"I'm afraid Jason might try to find his father when he turns 18. That wouldn't be good. I don't want to get his father in trouble. So I'm thinking maybe. . .maybe I should help him find his dad and arrange for a private meeting or something. I don't even know why I'm talking to you, except that if you live there, maybe you know him, and maybe you know if this is a good idea. I'm so confused and afraid!"

Verdene was obviously trying not to cry, and Skye knew it was time to step in.

"Your son's father—is his name Ezra Yoder?"

Verdene's eyes grew wide. She was as shocked as Skye had expected her to be.

"Yes," she said, leaning forward toward Skye. "But. . .how did you know?"

"He came to talk to me a few weeks ago, and told me the same story. He wants to meet his son."

Verdene stared at Skye in silence, and then the tears began coursing down her cheeks.

"He did? He does? But why? Why did he come talk to you?"

"That's another long story," Skye sighed. "Let's just say that I'm adopted and am just now getting to know my biological mother. I guess Ezra saw me as someone who could understand some of the feelings he's had, and his longing to meet his son."

Verdene sat quietly again, and Skye knew her words were still sinking in. Verdene had come to her on a spur-of-the-moment urge, and now she was being faced with an answer much quicker than she could have dreamed. Now there was no turning back. The realization of the unknowns ahead of her had to be heavy.

"Are you married? Do you have other children?" Skye asked.

Verdene shook her head no.

"Ezra is married and has five kids. He's never told his wife about you or his son."

"How did he know I had a boy?"

"He read it in the paper. He was surprised to see that you hadn't given the baby up for adoption because he thought that was the agreement." The words were out before Skye could stop them, and then she wondered if they were too harsh.

"I know. That's the other reason I've never contacted him. I broke my part of the promise. I chose to keep Jason, so I decided

I'd have to live with that decision. I didn't want to bother Ezra."

"But he's responsible for Jason too! You never thought about going back to him for child support?"

Verdene shook her head sideways again.

"And now you're ready to see him again, and have Jason meet him?"

"Yes. No. I don't know. I've bothered you enough already. I guess you can tell him I talked to you. Do you want my phone number?" Verdene was suddenly in a hurry to leave.

"I'll talk to him," Skye promised. "And I'll call you."

※ ※ ※

Bo and Skye talked about the unexpected turn of events as they drove home to Vicksburg.

"What if I hadn't agreed to do that concert?" Skye said.

"Not only that, but what if Mary Lou would have listened to the part of her that said it wasn't even worth trying to get you to come," Bo added. "She told us tonight she picked up the phone more than once to call you and then hung up when she lost her nerve."

"I know. It's amazing. And Verdene works for the same company, and was at the picnic. Even at that, she wouldn't have had to come talk to me."

"But she did, and now you know where Ezra's son is. It'll get more interesting from here on. I just hope nobody gets hurt too badly in this whole process."

"What do you mean?" Skye asked, even though she knew what her husband was talking about. Her mother had warned her about the same things.

"You know—Ezra, Lizzie and the kids, Jason, Verdene. These reunions don't always have happy endings. But you've gotta give it a try, honey. Maybe if God's been involved in getting it this far, God will help the rest work out too."

Skye smiled to herself. Bo talking about God. He didn't do that very often. She knew he believed in his heart, but talking about it wasn't easy for him. The evening's events must have really made an impact on him.

"We have to believe that everything will work out," she agreed. "You know, Romans 8:28."

Bo turned to stare at her in the darkness of their car. "All right, Miss Mennonite scholar, I don't know Romans 8:28. Enlighten me, please."

Skye giggled softly. "'All things work together for good for those who love the Lord and are called according to his purpose.' I had to memorize a lot of verses as a kid so I could earn my way to a week of camp."

"I've never heard of that before."

"Yeah, there were two ways to get to camp—pay your way, or memorize verses. 'Pay or pray' we kids called it, because we said we'd have to pray that we'd remember all those verses. Lots of kids' parents paid their way, but not ours. They wanted us to learn the verses. Especially Dad. That's the way he went to camp, and that's the way he wanted us to go too."

"How many verses did you have to learn?"

"Lots. I don't remember. Angela was a whiz at it, but it was hard for me. I remember practicing and practicing with her. She had so much patience with me."

"And you still remember the verses."

"More than I thought I would."

"So, if we had kids, would we make them do it?"

"I don't think the Mennonites in Kansas have the same kind of incentive with their camps."

"Well, then, there obviously wouldn't be any reason to try it."

Skye looked at Bo. She knew from the tone of his voice that he was half-joking and half-serious.

"I suppose we could tie it in with other privileges, like eating or going to the bathroom," she teased back. "You know, recite a verse and then you get breakfast. One more, and you can have the key to the bathroom."

Bo chuckled low in his throat. "Sounds like another good reason for us not to have kids. Not only would they have names like Hananiah and Zoephia, but they'd hate the Bible forever because of our memorization tactics."

Skye laughed too. They rode in silence for a while, and then she said, "I have been thinking that we might end up with a part-time kid."

"A part-time kid?"

"What if Jason comes to visit Ezra but he needs a place to stay other than at Ezra's house?"

"I hadn't thought about that."

"Our place would be logical. People are already used to Ezra coming over a lot, even though they don't know why."

"Sure, it makes sense. Are you going to suggest that to Ezra?"

"I think so."

"When?"

"I'm sure he'll stop by in the next day or so."

"You're probably right."

🙢 🙢 🙢

Ezra didn't stop by for the next few days, and Skye was starting to wonder why. Maybe he'd gotten cold feet. Wouldn't that be great, now that she'd found Jason. Or maybe he was busy and just didn't have time.

When his buggy did roll into their yard almost a week after the concert, Skye was in the middle of a phone conversation with Jake in New York. Why did that always happen? she wondered, listening to Jake as she watched Ezra come up the porch steps. The doorbell rang.

"Hey, Jake, my Amish friend is back again," she said. "Can

we wrap this up for now and I'll call you a little bit later?"

"I don't know, Skye, I'm starting to feel like I'm being replaced by an Amish man," Jake joked. "You aren't secretly producing Amish music videos with him, are you?"

Skye laughed and assured Jake she'd bring him up-to-date on the saga of Ezra the next time she sent him an e-mail. Jake reminded her that she didn't have much time to learn the songs before their scheduled recording sessions in New York. Skye said yes, yes, and promised she'd be ready.

Clicking off the phone, Skye went to the door. She opened it to find Ezra sitting on the top step with Zebediah beside him.

"Hi, Ezra," she said. "Sorry to keep you waiting, but I was on the phone."

"No problem. I was just having a little talk with Zeb."

"Do you want to come in?"

"Sure."

"Let's sit here," Skye indicated the kitchen booth. She poured glasses of tea for them, remembering to put the sugar bowl on the table for Ezra. She set a plate of chocolate-chip cookies between them, and sat down.

"Something very unusual happened last Saturday that I need to tell you about," she began.

Ezra

EZRA
ONE

Ezra Yoder listened intently as Skye told him about Verdene coming to see her after the concert in Vicksburg. A strange combination of fear and relief flooded through him, and he felt his stomach doing weird things. What he'd hoped for was within reach—meeting the son he'd never known. That part he could live with. It was the exposure of his teenage sin that scared him half-to-death. It was the knowing that when this got out, he would never be able to look into the faces of his Amish friends and relatives without reading judgment in their eyes.

Then why was he doing this?

He'd asked himself that question many times, both before and after he'd approached Skye about it the first time. And, after much soul-searching, the answer came back the same: If you were that boy, wouldn't you want to know your father? Don't you owe at least that much to him?

I am Amish, Ezra had told himself. And Amish put the family in a very important place in their lives. The boy he had fathered as a drunken teenager was still his son. He simply couldn't go through his life knowing that he had "family" out there, somewhere, that he didn't know, and that didn't know him.

That's why he was doing this.

Ironically, his Amish traditions were driving him to this decision, and yet it was the Amish he feared the most in the process. They would talk. Oh, would they talk! He could hear it now.

"Can you believe it? Ezra Yoder's got an English son."

"Yeah, what must this be doing to poor Lizzie?"

"I always did think he seemed a little strange—like he had a secret."

"What's he going to do now?'

The whispers would float from household to household, gaining gossip until, weighted down with truths and half-truths, the burden would fall squarely on his shoulders—where it belonged, after all. It was his mistake. Now he was paying for it.

Ezra looked at Skye, and he saw deep concern in her eyes.

"Do you want me to call Verdene and set up a time for you to meet her and Jason?"

"I guess so," he sighed. "Where?"

"How about here?"

"That would be okay."

"When?"

When. When would be a good time to do this? To take the step that would change everything. Sooner, later, did it matter? And when would he tell Lizzie? Before or after he met Jason?

He couldn't decide.

"Any time except Sunday," he finally muttered, finishing the last of the tea in his glass.

"It'll have to be in the evening unless it's on Saturday, because Verdene works during the day," Skye said. "Would you like some more tea?"

"No, I need to be going. Just let me know." He stood up and began walking toward the door. He picked up his straw hat from the chair where he'd laid it, and then looked at Skye, who'd followed him to the door. "Do you think I'm doing the right thing?" he asked.

She reached out and touched his shoulder lightly. "Yes, I do.

But the right thing isn't always the easy thing."

He put his hat on. He wanted to say something more, but he didn't know what, or how. So he just nodded and walked out the door.

🙠 🙠 🙠

Ezra drove his horse and buggy onto his farmyard, hardly noticing that he was home. The horse knew the way, and took itself and the buggy to the family hitching post near the barn. Ezra climbed out of the buggy, tied the horse to the post, and began unhitching the buggy. His son Cris was soon there, helping on the other side of the horse.

"Where'd you go, Dad?" Cris wanted to know.

"To town."

"What'd you get?"

"Some wormer for the sheep."

"That's all?"

"I got some wormer because the sheep are starting to look like they need it, and decided to get some for Bo's sheep too while I was at it. Is that okay with you?" Ezra found himself getting impatient with his son, and he didn't like it. But he didn't feel like answering a lot of questions either. He really had gone to Wellsford, bought wormer, and had intended to give some to Bo and Skye. The fact that he forgot to leave it there made him feel really stupid.

"Did you see Zeb at Bo's?" Cris asked.

"Yah, he's doing fine. Here, take Sally to the pasture," Ezra handed the horse's lead rope to his son.

Ezra got the bottle of sheep wormer out of the buggy and walked toward the barn. He put the bottle in the cupboard with his other sheep medications and supplies. Tomorrow morning, he and Cris would take care of that. Now, it was time to milk the cows. He could hear Lizzie bringing them into the holding pen, where they'd wait their turn to come into the barn.

Ezra hurried to the house to change clothes, and was soon back in the barn. Lizzie had the first group of cows in the milking parlor, and was putting the milkers on the first cow. She looked up at Ezra and smiled faintly.

"I was starting to wonder where you were," she said, her face glistening with sweat. Her traditional white head covering had been replaced by a dark blue handkerchief for choring, and her dress was faded and worn. She was barefoot.

"I got some wormer in Wellsford and stopped to leave some at Bo's," Ezra said.

"Oh," Lizzie said, her face next to the big Holstein's belly. "Are their sheep bad too?"

"I figured if ours are, theirs probably are too. They don't know anything about sheep. I'm just trying to help them get started."

"You must be doing a really good job," Lizzie said, and Ezra heard suspicion in her voice.

"What do you mean?" he went over to stand near her.

"Nothing."

"Yes you do. What do you mean, Lizzie?"

"People are starting to talk, Ezra. You're over there a lot. People are wondering why you go to Skye and Bo's all the time."

Ezra's heart sank. He'd have to tell Lizzie soon. Might as well get it over with.

"I'll tell you all about it, Liz, after the kids are in bed tonight, okay?"

His wife looked at him, her eyes full of questions. She simply said "okay" and went on to the next cow.

Except for when the children came in to talk, they didn't say a word to each other during the rest of the chores. Ezra was rehearsing how to tell Lizzie his story, and he could imagine what she was thinking. She was probably afraid he was having an affair with Skye.

No, his affair had been a long time ago. Now he had to tell his wife about the consequences.

      🌿 🌿 🌿

The tension hung heavy between Ezra and Lizzie all evening—as heavy as the humidity that clung to their clothes and bodies. Ezra was glad to hear the rumble of thunder in the distance—maybe they'd get a rain during the night that would take some of the moisture out of the air. The crops and garden could sure use it too.

The children were finally in bed, although Cris insisted he wouldn't be able to sleep. He'd been afraid of thunderstorms ever since the one that spooked his horses in Wellsford, leaving him with a badly broken leg. The leg was healing, but Ezra wondered if Cris would have permanent scars of fear. Thunderstorms were common in Kansas. It wouldn't be good for Cris to grow up in terror of them. A healthy respect, yes, but not an irrational fright.

Ezra and Lizzie sat on their screened-in porch in the dark. They didn't need light to talk, and the propane lamp would only add more heat to a hot evening.

"There's something I've never told you or anyone—something that happened when I was 16," Ezra began. "I was at a party. I got drunk. I don't remember it, but I was with a girl named Verdene Johnson. Two months later she told me she was pregnant, and it was my baby." Ezra paused. He heard Lizzie suck in her breath sharply and say, "Oh, my goodness."

"We agreed that she would put the baby up for adoption, but I found out she didn't. I read the paper when the baby was born—it was a boy."

Lizzie sat beside him quietly in the darkness.

"When I heard about Skye being adopted, I went to talk to her. I told her about the baby. After talking to her, I decided I wanted to meet my boy."

"Was that her idea? Did she talk you into that?" Lizzie

sounded angry.

"No, no, no. She said she would help me if I wanted to, but I was the one who wanted to do it."

"So that's why you're always going to see her."

"Yes."

Silence hung between them before Ezra continued.

"I found out today that Skye knows where Verdene and my boy are."

Ezra went on to tell the story of Verdene coming to Skye's concert and seeking her out afterward. "She's going to set up a time for me to meet them," he concluded.

Then he waited. Ezra knew his wife of twelve years pretty well, but he wasn't sure how she would react to this news. This was the first time in their marriage that something so serious had come between them.

Suddenly Lizzie stood up, stomped off the porch, and began running into the darkness of the farmyard. Ezra got up to follow, but stopped when he heard his wife's cries of anger and anguish drift back toward him.

He had never heard those noises come from her before. He'd seen sadness, and he'd seen frustration. But he'd never seen or heard Lizzie carry on like she was now. A stab of pain seared through Ezra, as if the heart attack that had hit his own father at 45 was now coming to claim him. What horrible thing had he done to his wife?

Ezra followed Lizzie's cries to a large elm tree near the barn. She was leaning into it, pounding her fists into the gnarly bark, crying and cursing. She was cursing him.

"Lizzie. . ."

"Don't touch me, Ezra. After twelve years of marriage, I find out you had a baby with another woman," she spit the words at him in the darkness. "It's not a very nice surprise."

"I know. I'm sorry, but. . ."

"Don't 'but' me, Ezra," she interrupted. "What I want to know is what else you did when you were too drunk to remember? Are there others?"

"No, no, no!"

"How can I ever trust you again?"

"Honest, Lizzie, I have never betrayed you! This all happened before I even knew you!"

"But why didn't you tell me?"

"I don't know. I guess I thought it was in the past, and it would always be left there."

"And then who decides to bring it up from the past? YOU DO!"

"I know." Ezra felt like he'd gone through a physical beating.

"So, where are you going to meet him?" Lizzie threw the question at Ezra. "Are you going to bring this son of yours here and say to our children, 'Oh, by the way, your daddy has another boy he forgot to tell us about. Meet your brother Jason.' Is that what you're gonna do?"

"No. Skye and Bo offered that we could meet at their place," Ezra said quietly.

"And what happens after the first time? Then what?"

"I don't know, Lizzie. I don't know."

"Well, you should've thought about it before you got us all into this mess." Lizzie brushed past him and headed toward the house.

Ezra hurt so bad inside, he wondered if he would ever feel good again. He'd expected Lizzie to be upset. But he'd been hoping against hope that she could somehow forgive him and walk with him through this experience. Obviously, that wasn't going to be the case. No one—no one except Skye and Bo—understood him and would stand beside him.

EZRA

TWO

Ezra almost didn't turn his horse into Bo and Skye's lane that first evening in September. He wanted to just keep on driving until...until he'd left the past and the present behind him, and all he'd have to face would be the future. But he knew that wasn't possible. He cued Sally with a slight flick of his wrist, sending the message along the reins and to the bit in her mouth. She made the turn and clip-clopped down the familiar driveway.

Zeb saw the horse and buggy coming and ran to meet them, barking excitedly at the rolling wooden wheels. Zeb loved company, especially Ezra.

By the time Ezra had stopped his horse at the hitching post and stepped out of his buggy, Zeb was standing beside him with a stick in his mouth. Zeb, like many border collies, had a significant addiction to retrieving. Given the opportunity to chase a stick or frisbee and bring it back, Zeb would wear out the interest of the thrower long before he would lose interest in the game himself. Ezra was usually good for at least a few throws.

But this evening, Ezra barely noticed the bright-eyed black-and-white dog waiting for him. Ezra's eyes were on the late-model car sitting in front of Bo and Skye's house. Verdene's car. His heart jumped.

Zeb nudged Ezra's leg, and Ezra looked down at him. He'd

give anything today to be as carefree as that dog. He took the stick out of Zeb's mouth and tossed it away with trembling hands.

The front door of the house opened. Skye stepped out, followed by a woman and teenage boy. So, here they were.

Ezra made his way toward the porch, ignoring the dog prancing beside him with the retrieved stick. His heart was doing a dance of its own as Ezra reached the steps.

"Ezra, this is Verdene and Jason," he heard Skye say.

He shook the hand of the attractive woman. He would have never recognized her as the mother of his son. Painfully, he realized that probably had more to do with the circumstances of their tryst than the fact that she was seventeen years older than the last time he had seen her.

He shook the hand of the boy. It was an uncertain handshake—not hard and strong like the Amish boys he knew. "Jason," he said, "it's good to meet you."

"You too," Jason muttered.

What does a man say when he's meeting his teenage son for the first time? Ezra hoped desperately that Skye, or Verdene, or someone would fill in the space between them.

Zeb had of course followed Ezra up onto the porch, the stick still in his mouth. Ezra saw Jason watching the dog.

"He wants somebody to throw the stick so he can bring it back," Ezra said. "Here." He took the small branch from Zeb and gave it to Jason.

The tall lanky boy stepped off of the porch and walked several yards away from the house. Zeb, who had eyes only for the twig, followed him. Jason threw the stick high into the air, and Zeb was off.

But he didn't go far, because Zeb had seen this play before. He knew about sticks that went far, and sticks that went high. The far ones he had to run like the dickens to catch in mid-air. But the high ones were easy—he just had to wait for the stick to come down.

Ezra, Verdene, Jason, and Skye watched as Zeb grabbed the stick before it hit the ground, and Ezra saw a slight smile cross Jason's face.

"Do you have a dog, Verdene?" Skye asked.

"No, we don't have room. But Jason has always wanted one."

Ezra studied his son as Jason continued to play with Zeb. They shared the same body build, the same straight dark brown hair. Jason's hair was long, and he kept tucking it behind his ears. Kinda hippie looking, Ezra thought. He wondered if Jason gave his mother problems.

There was so much he wanted to ask Verdene—so much he wanted to know about Jason. Was he smart in school? What did he like to do? What had she told him about his father? Were they religious people?

"I'll get some drinks and cookies, and we can go sit on the deck," Skye said.

≈ ≈ ≈

Two hours later, Ezra left, the battery-powered lights on his buggy blinking red in the back, shining white in the front. He didn't know how the two hours had passed so easily, but they had, with Skye and Bo helping the conversation along. He knew a lot more about Verdene and Jason and their lives for the last seventeen years, and they knew more about him too. It hadn't been so bad after all, this first meeting.

Ezra noticed lights down the road when he stopped Sally at the end of the lane, but they were dim—buggy lights, not car lights. They weren't coming very fast, so he turned Sally out into the road and set her in the steady pace she'd keep for the short trip home. The lights behind him didn't seem to be gaining, but as he looked back, he noticed there seemed to be more than one set. He wondered where all of the buggies would be leaving from at the same time. Probably a family get-together at the Weavers down the road, he mused.

He hadn't gone far before Ezra felt doubts and depression replacing the good feelings he'd had about meeting Jason. Here he was, leaving a son he'd fathered years ago with a woman he didn't know, to go home to a life he had created with the wife he loved. He was glad Lizzie and the children weren't home—they'd gone to visit relatives in Garden Town for the weekend. He didn't know how he would have been able to face them or talk to them that evening.

In fact, the more he thought about it, the more he couldn't face himself. What had he done? His wife—the only woman he had ever loved—was acting like she hated him. "What kind of influence is this on our children?" she'd asked. "How can you tell them to be good when you've done this?"

Her relatives and the rest of the community would side with her, of course. He was alone. The friendship of Skye and Bo didn't mean much if he didn't have his family and his church.

Maybe he should just leave. Not be there when the family got back. They would all be shocked, but they'd get through it. Their relatives and church people would help them out.

But he couldn't do that. He couldn't leave his kids. And besides, where would he go? He couldn't join another Amish community because the word would get out about him. And he couldn't leave the Amish—then he'd be shunned for sure. Outcast—he was destined to live the rest of his days as an outcast. And that's what he deserved for upsetting Lizzie and putting her and his family into this situation.

❦ ❦ ❦

It didn't happen overnight. No, rumor mills need more time than that. More time, and more fodder.

This one had begun grinding its gossip weeks earlier, when, like Lizzie had explained to Ezra, "People are starting to talk—

they're wondering why you go to Skye and Bo's all the time."

The evening that Ezra went to meet Verdene and Jason, the Weaver family had a big birthday gathering. Some of them were in the buggies that saw Ezra leave Bo's place. The rumor mill had something new to chew on.

"Isn't this the weekend Lizzie and the kids went to see their relatives in Garden Town?" Hattie Weaver said to her sister Erma, who nodded her white-capped head. "And we saw Ezra coming out of Bo's yard late at night. What do you suppose. . ." she let the sentence trail off under her raised eyebrows.

Erma mentioned it to Inez Keim, who said her husband saw Ezra stopping in there "all the time, during the day, when Bo's at work."

Inez said something to Mary Miller, who rolled her eyes and said she always did wonder about that Skye, no offense to her grandfather Jonas or anything, but have you seen what she wears when she goes out walking in the morning?

Mary Miller asked her husband, Leon, if he thought Ezra was the type to have an affair with a worldly woman, and Leon said he didn't think so, but Ezra was a hard man to read.

Leon was over at his brother Amos's house one day. Although Amos wasn't home, his wife Aldina was, and Leon brought up the topic. Aldina happened to be Lizzie's sister, and Leon figured she just might know something. Aldina didn't have much to say to Leon, but privately, she resolved to find out if Lizzie knew anything the next time they were together.

And when Lizzie's sister Aldina said, "Ezra sure seems to spend a lot of time over at Skye's," Lizzie had had enough. She was tired of hearing the innuendos, now even from her own sister. She told Aldina the truth. The truth was that Skye had helped Ezra find a son he'd fathered as a teenager.

Aldina wanted to keep the secret Lizzie had shared, but not from her husband, of course. Amos laughed loud and long, saying he remembered that party himself. And then he grew serious and said it sure was too bad Ezra got himself in trouble that night.

Amos didn't mean to, but he kinda let it slip to some of the Amish men at the Wellsford Hardware store one day. Some of them had been at that party too, and he couldn't resist rehashing their years as "young folks" and the crazy things they did. The men even joked about whether any of them might have kids "out there" like Ezra did. "Beware of English women who want to talk to you," Leon joked, and everybody laughed.

And so the word got out. Ezra Yoder has an English son that he's been in contact with, thanks to the help of Skye and Bo. Poor Lizzie is fit to be tied, and the kids don't even know yet.

※ ※ ※

There was no turning back now, and Ezra saw it in the faces of his community. People knew. He hadn't told anyone, and Lizzie said the only person she told was her sister, and Aldina wouldn't tell.

It didn't matter. He knew it couldn't stay hidden forever.

But they had to tell the children—soon. Before they heard it from the kids in school.

And so they sat down with the children one evening after supper. Ezra knew he'd have to do all of the explaining—the most he could hope for from Lizzie was silence. Any words she might add would probably be angry and bitter. He didn't know how to say what he had to say, except to just come out and explain as best he could to children too young to understand the hows and whys of illegitimate babies.

The children sat in a row on the living room couch—Cris, Benjamin, Bethany, and Sarah. Little Marcus sat on Lizzie's lap, gurgling and drooling.

"I need to tell you all something," Ezra began, fidgeting under the gazes of his children. "You all. . .you all have a brother that you've never known about."

"A *brother*?" Cris asked.

"Yes, a 17-year-old half-brother."

"Where?" eight-year-old Benjamin wondered.

"He lives in Vicksburg with his mother."

Silence. Ezra knew they were trying to figure this one out.

"Have you been married before?" Cris asked.

"No, no, no. I. . .I had a baby with a girl when I was just 16—a long time before your mommy and I got married."

Silence. Just a row of blue eyes looking at him.

"His name is Jason. I've met him once. Would you like to meet him?"

"Sure," Cris said. The others nodded quietly.

"Is he Amish?" five-year-old Bethany wondered.

"No, he's not."

"Why not?" Bethany again.

"It's a long story," Ezra said, thinking that it really was a very short story.

"Is he coming over here? Does he ride horses?" Benjamin was planning things to do with his newfound brother.

"I doubt that he rides horses—he hasn't had a chance, living in Vicksburg. He likes dogs though!"

Ezra saw Cris and Benjamin exchange looks. A teenage boy who liked dogs wasn't very exciting.

"Does he have a bike?" Cris asked.

"I don't know," Ezra said. Bicycles weren't allowed in their Wellsford Amish community. Cris was hoping a bike would be part of the new-brother deal.

"When's he coming to visit us?" Benjamin repeated the question his father had ignored earlier.

"I don't know that either. We just wanted to tell you about him, because you will probably be hearing about it from other kids. They might say bad things about me."

"What bad things?" Benjamin's innocent blue eyes searched his father's face.

"We don't know what you might hear," Lizzie finally spoke. "But you come home and tell us, okay?"

Three young heads nodded solemnly. Three-year-old Sarah, watching her siblings, looked back at her parents and nodded too.

"Now can we go play?" Bethany wondered.

"No, now you can go get ready for bed," Lizzie answered. She stood up with Marcus in one arm and reached for Sarah's small hand. "Come, Sarah, let's go take a bath."

Ezra watched as his wife and children left the room. Long after the children had taken their baths and been tucked in for the night, he still sat in the recliner. The occasional heartache he'd felt when he was deciding whether or not to meet his son had been replaced by a constant heartbreak. Maybe he and Jason had some sort of future as a father and son. But what was this going to do to his other children? What would the community gossip put in their tender ears?

"What kind of example are you for your children? How can you ever teach them right from wrong? What will you tell Cris when he turns 16?" Lizzie's words rang in his ears and echoed through his soul.

Was he destroying his relationship with his other children in the process of building one with Jason? Then it would never, never be worth it.

A huge sadness dropped over Ezra like a wet blanket.

EZRA

THREE

H E KNEW HE WASN'T the most upbeat, cheerful man in the world. It just wasn't in him. He got it from his mom, he guessed. She'd always been the moody type.

But for the majority of his life, Ezra had been able to keep his head above water. He was glad for Lizzie and the kids. They took his attention away from himself when he had a tendency to get depressed. The kids especially helped him fill the emptiness inside of him.

Church didn't help. Well, maybe when Jonas Bontrager preached, it was okay. He could listen to Jonas and get something out of it. The other ministers. . .well, the best way to pass the time was to doze. Which he'd had less chance to do now that they had Marcus. He and Lizzie took turns taking care of their youngest son during the three-hour service. The men sat in one part of the house and the women in another part for the worship service, and when Lizzie had Marcus, Bethany and Sara helped entertain him. Ezra had Cris and Benjamin with him, so they helped babysit too.

The second Sunday in September, church was scheduled to be at their house. More stress. He should have thought about that when he agreed to meet Jason on the first of the month. But he hadn't. And now, on top of everything else, he had to get his house, farm, and barn ready to host 30 families for church.

He and Lizzie didn't have to do it alone. Family members always helped each other get ready for church—the women cleaning the house from top to bottom, the men working in the barn. This was usually an enjoyable time together because they passed the time talking and telling jokes, and when it was over, it felt good to have everything so clean and orderly.

But Ezra worried about this year. One of two things would happen. Either the relatives would spend the days avoiding the issue of Jason, small-talking their way around what they all were wondering about, or they would come right out and ask him.

He didn't know which would be worse.

         ✥ ✥ ✥

As it turned out, they did both. For two days, family members came and went, getting the farm ready to host church. They sat around the table together and talked about everything else. Then, the last evening, while the kids were outside playing, after the women had washed the dishes and joined the men in the living room, Aldina brought it up.

"I think we should talk about this thing with Ezra's English boy," she began, looking at her sister Lizzie briefly. "We're family, and we're very concerned. Lizzie looks like she's aged ten years in the last week, and I, for one, am worried about her. We should know what's going on," Aldina's eyes settled on Ezra.

Amazing how quiet a room can get, Ezra thought, shifting uncomfortably in a chair. He looked at Lizzie. Yes, she did look like she was carrying the weight of the world on her shoulders. It was all his fault.

"I don't know what to say that you haven't all heard already," Ezra hung his head, studying the wooden floor.

"We may have heard things, but we want to hear the real story from you," Aldina prodded.

Ezra took a deep breath and ran his hand through his straight black hair. "The real story is pretty simple. I got drunk at a party when I was 16, slept with an English girl named Verdene Johnson, and she got pregnant. We'd agreed she would give the baby up for adoption, but she decided to keep him. I knew about it because I read it in the paper. This summer I decided I wanted to know this son of mine, and I told Skye Martin because she's been through sorta the same thing with her mother. Verdene ended up talking to Skye after a concert she did in Vicksburg, and that's how it all happened. I've seen the boy once—his name is Jason. His mother never married and they live in Vicksburg. That's about it."

"Why did you do this? Why didn't you leave well enough alone?" Aldina's husband, Amos, asked.

It was a question he'd asked himself lately too, Ezra admitted to himself, but aloud he answered, "Imagine if you knew you had a son or daughter somewhere. Wouldn't you do the same?"

Silence. Then Amos muttered, "I wouldn't have got myself in trouble like that."

Fire flew through Ezra's mind, and he almost exploded. Yeah, right, Amos, he fumed. You just didn't get caught. Don't pull that "holier than thou" stuff on me.

But he didn't say anything. What good would it do?

"So what now? Now that you've met him?" Aldina again.

"I'm not sure. I think I'd like to get to know him. I can't do anything about the past, but I can about the future," Ezra heard himself saying, and he sounded more positive than he felt.

"Well, it's the actions of the past that are making this mess for us, and I don't know what that means for the future of me and the kids," Lizzie spoke, bitterness dripping from her words. "I wish I'd known this years ago."

Ezra cringed. The implications of her words stabbed deep.

"What do your kids say about this?" Lizzie's other sister, Ruth, asked.

"They're curious. They want to meet Jason."

Silence. Ezra's eyes traveled around the room. More than half of the people there hadn't said a word. The men were sitting, arms crossed, long beards resting on their chests, eyes on the floor or somewhere on the wall. The women in their white coverings and dark dresses sat staring at folded hands in their laps.

"I think you should stop this before it goes any farther," Amos said. "You've met the boy. Now leave him behind and take care of your family. It's bad enough as it is. You'll probably have to answer to the deacon and the ministers. Confess to them, then go on."

Outside, a child began to cry, and soon the youngster was in the house, running for the comfort of her mother's lap. Several other children followed, explaining and tattling on each other. It appeared the family meeting was over.

❦ ❦ ❦

He still didn't know why he did it, but he had to admit, he felt better after talking to Skye. He'd taken the sheep wormer over to her place, and when she asked how things were going, he'd started talking and he couldn't stop. Before he knew it, he'd unloaded everything about his kids, Lizzie, the relatives, the people gossiping. He'd told her he was wondering if he should have ever done this, and asking her what he should do now.

Skye had said she still thought he'd done the right thing. She'd said her parents got a lot of flak from their Mennonite community when they adopted the twins. "But they knew it was what God had called them to do," Skye said.

Ezra didn't know what to think about that God talk. He couldn't say he felt God had told him to find his son. He couldn't honestly say he thought God had ever told him to do anything. The Amish religion told him how to dress and which lifestyle rules to follow, but God?

God judged people. God's judgment resulted in punishment,

and he was probably being punished now for the sins of his youth. That's as much of God as he could see in this situation.

Several days after their talk, Skye and Bo stopped in at Ezra's place just as the family was sitting down for supper. They hardly ever came over, and Ezra wondered what was up. He went to the door and saw Skye standing there with an envelope in her hand.

"Hi, Ezra," Skye said. "I wanted to bring this over to you—it's an e-mail I got this morning that was addressed to you."

E-mail? Addressed to him?

"It's self-explanatory when you read it," Skye answered his unasked questions.

"Okay. Thank-you."

"No problem. Talk to you later."

And with that, she was back on the big cycle with Bo and they were roaring out of the yard.

Ezra returned to the family table. "They had some mail there that belonged to me," he said simply.

🌿 🌿 🌿

Ezra opened the envelope as soon as the children were gone from the supper table. He unfolded the white paper inside.

"Who's it from?" Lizzie asked, watching intently.

Ezra read the note Skye had written on top of the page, then read it out loud to his wife: "I hope it's okay, but I told my mother about the things you're going through, thinking that she might have some advice. She sent this answer back."

"What did you tell Skye?" Lizzie demanded.

"I just told her how it's been hard to live with the gossip and all."

"When was that?"

"When I took the wormer over the other day."

Lizzie got up from the table and began to clear it off. She was obviously upset that he'd talked to Skye.

Ezra read the letter silently:

Dear Ezra,
    Although I don't know you, I felt like I wanted to write you after Skye told me what you're going through. My husband, Ken, and I had to face people who didn't support our decision to adopt Skye and Angela, so I kinda know how you must be feeling.
    It hurts a lot to have people talking about you and saying negative things, I know. One thing that I remember my Amish grandma saying to me when I was a little girl, and I got hurt and was crying, was this: "When you are a grandma like me, you won't even remember where it hurt." Since then, I've read something that someone else wrote, saying that we should think about things in terms of if it will matter a year from now.
    A year from now, what will be most important—that you know your son Jason or that people talked about you?
    A year from now, what will matter—that you followed your heart or that your heart experienced some pain in the process?
    I can't answer those questions for you, but maybe they will give you some perspective during these trying times.

May God be with you,
Becca Bontrager Martin

He handed the letter to Lizzie, and she read it immediately.
"What do you think?" Ezra asked.
"Easy for her to say. Especially since there was nothing *wrong* about adopting those girls."
"And it was wrong for me to find Jason?"
Lizzie was silent, and Ezra knew exactly what she wouldn't

say out loud. Jason's presence in their lives would always remind her that Ezra had known another woman intimately before he married her. He doubted that his relationship with his wife would ever be the same again. And it hurt. It hurt bad.

EZRA
FOUR

EZRA HAD DREADED SUNDAY, and rightly so. Hosting 30 Amish families in his home for church was an ordeal enough under normal circumstances. Knowing that he would be the focus of whisperings and sidelong glances made it a nightmare.

But he survived. And, at the end of the afternoon, when the deacon came up to him in private and said he and the bishop wanted to come over sometime soon to talk with him, Ezra was almost relieved. He'd been expecting their visit—he might as well get it over with.

They didn't waste any time. Monday evening, the clop-clop-clop of a horse's hooves on Ezra's lane drew the attention of his family just as they were finishing supper. Cris jumped up from the table to look out the window.

"It's Bishop Wenger," he announced, "and somebody else."

Ezra's stomach flipped. "Light the lamp in your room and take Ben, Bethany, and Sarah up with you. Play some games with them," he instructed Cris.

It took a few minutes for Bishop Wenger and Deacon Schrock to tie up the horse. During that time, the family hastily cleaned off the table, then Cris took the children to the bedroom he shared with Ben. Ezra knew Cris would keep them occupied for awhile. He went to the door and opened it just as Bishop

Wenger was about to knock.

"Good evening, Ezra."

"Good evening. Come in."

"Thank-you."

Ezra moved the lamp from the kitchen, where they'd been using it for supper, into the living room. Lizzie followed him and sat down in her rocker. Bishop Wenger and Deacon Schrock found places on the couch, and Ezra sat down heavily in his recliner. He waited.

"You know why we are here, I suppose," the stocky bishop in his mid-50's began.

Ezra nodded.

"Maybe, before we go any further, you should tell us about this English son of yours, and why you have decided to get in contact with him."

Ezra repeated the story he was getting tired of telling—especially since the responses were always the same. This time, the listeners could do more than throw negative words or stunned silence at him. These men had the power to discipline him.

"So you have met this son, and you plan to keep on seeing him?" Bishop Wenger asked.

Ezra studied the braided rug at his feet. "I thought I would, yes," he said quietly.

"We don't think that is a good idea," Deacon Schrock stated. Ezra looked up to see the deacon's dark eyes penetrating his. Deacon Schrock never beat around the bush. Some people said he enjoyed his role as disciplinarian in the church—that he got a kick out of telling people they needed to shape up. Ezra could almost believe it.

"You sinned when you got that girl pregnant," Deacon Schrock continued. "Bringing it all out into the open now makes it worse. Now your sin is affecting not only you but also your wife and your children too. Forget about that boy. His mother has raised him this far, and she will keep on taking care of him. He doesn't need you. Your responsibility is to the family God gave you in your marriage—your sacred marriage."

Ezra heard a sob coming from Lizzie.

"Your wife and your family are the most important things," Bishop Wenger picked up where Deacon Schrock left off. "Anything that gets in between you and them is wrong. Something *has* come between you and them. For that, there should be confession."

Confession. In front of the whole church. Ezra hung his head low, his black beard resting on his chest.

"Are you prepared to confess?" Bishop Wenger's voice had softened.

"Yes."

"And are you prepared to forget about this English son, to put the past behind you, and go forward without looking back?" Deacon Schrock asked.

Ezra could not answer that question. Not now. He needed time.

"I will confess what I have done. I cannot say yet what I will do," he replied.

"Jesus said to the woman caught in adultery, 'Go and sin no more,'" Deacon Schrock admonished. "What good is confession if there is not a change in your heart?"

Ezra had no answer. He could not argue with the men. He could only hope that between now and the time of his confession at the next church service, he would know what to do.

ॐ ॐ ॐ

When the thought first crossed his mind, he put it away immediately. No. He couldn't do that.

He remembered an Amish woman who'd committed suicide in the community when he was a teenager. He remembered the funeral—so much loud, anguished crying. Suicide was a sin. She had committed a final sin that would condemn her to hell forever. The ministers offered no hope for her soul, but used her as an example to the congregation. "The road to hell is wide and short, and many will be on it," they preached. "The road to heaven is long and narrow, and few will travel that way."

The only way for him was to give up the idea of seeing Jason again. Agree that it had been a mistake. Tell Skye to tell Verdene and Jason that he was sorry, but it just wasn't going to work out.

An autumn chill hung in the air the evening he went to tell Skye and Bo. It was a chill he felt deeply, and it was more than the Kansas wind pushing the coldness to his bones. He knocked on the door.

Bo opened it, and Ezra was glad. He liked this English man. He liked his sense of humor, his solid presence, his openness. Bo invited him in.

"Skye's packing—she leaves tomorrow for New York," Bo said. "Go ahead and have a seat. Skye! Ezra's stopped by."

"I don't want to bother you all if you're busy. . ."

"No problem."

"Hi, Ezra," Skye came into the room. "I'm glad you stopped by. We just got a call this evening from Verdene. Jason's wondering when he's going to see you again. She says that after the shock and newness wore off, he's intrigued with getting to know his Amish father better."

No. No. He did not need this.

"I. . .I was actually going to say that, well, that I don't want to see him again," Ezra fumbled with his hat he was holding in his hands.

"What? Why?" Skye's raised voice registered her surprise.

"It's better that way. Better for everybody."

"How's it better, Ezra?" Bo asked.

"It isn't fair to Lizzie and the kids," Ezra said, preferring to stay away from talking about the visit from the deacon and bishop and his upcoming confession. As much as he liked Bo and Skye, he didn't want to talk about the internal workings of his Amish church.

"And is it fair to Jason?" Skye wanted to know.

"No, and that's my fault. I should have never started this. I will pay for that."

"You may have started it, but so did Verdene. Remember?"

"Yes, but if I had never told you, you wouldn't have known it was me."

"And that's what says to me that God was a part of this," Skye said.

Ezra didn't want to hear that. He didn't know how to handle that kind of explanation about God's involvement. He was used to a God who punished—a God that called for confession, as explained by the deacon and bishop. What was he supposed to do now, with Skye saying that God had brought him and Jason together, and the church saying he needed to leave him behind?

"Look, Ezra, this God stuff is still new to me," Bo said. "But I can't help believe that there was a reason for all of this to come together like it did. And I can't see you just walking away from it all now."

They have no idea what I'm going through, Ezra agonized. The church, my family, my traditions are all telling me to do one thing. My heart, Bo and Skye, Jason and Verdene are saying another. There's no compromise. I have to decide one way or another. And either way, I lose.

"Look, Bo, Skye," he said. "For right now, don't call Verdene. Don't make any plans. I need time to think about it, okay?"

"Okay," Skye agreed, and Bo nodded his head yes.

Ezra knew they wanted to talk more about it, but he didn't want to.

"So, how are the sheep?" he asked. "Some of them should be lambing before long. Are they starting to show?"

"I don't know. How does a pregnant ewe look?" Skye asked.

"Seems to me they can hide a lot under that coat of wool."

"Yes, but you'll be able to tell when they get big from carrying a lamb. And you can watch the udders too."

"There's a job for you, Skye," Bo chuckled. "Watch those udders, and when they are full of milk, get your lambing kit ready."

Ezra chuckled too. He couldn't quite imagine Skye pulling a new lamb that the ewe was having trouble delivering, but she'd learn. Yes, she and Bo would learn.

"That reminds me. . .I've got a ewe that prolapsed, and I think I'm going to have to put her down. I don't have a gun. Bo, do you have a rifle I could borrow?"

"Sure," Bo said. "I'll get it."

Bo left, and returned shortly with the rifle. "Sorry about the ewe," he said as he handed the gun to Ezra. "I hope I don't ever have to shoot any of ours."

"It's not any fun, but sometimes it has to be done," Ezra said, standing up to leave. "If she's in misery, it's the best."

"Yeah, I know," Bo agreed.

"I'll let you know what I decide about Jason," Ezra said as he walked toward the door, cradling the rifle in his arm. "And I'll get the gun back to you soon."

"That'll be fine."

Ezra heard the door close behind him as he walked to his buggy. The gun felt strange in his hands. He'd never enjoyed hunting. Other Amish men hunted coyotes and deer, but it wasn't something he liked to do.

The ride home with the gun in his buggy lasted forever. The weapon lay on the floor at his feet. Cold. Hard. A machine built to kill. Ezra shuddered. Without really knowing why, he'd taken the first step. He had the gun. Part of him wanted to throw it out of the buggy as far as he could, afraid of what it represented. And part of him felt almost relieved to have it.

Sometimes it has to be done to end the misery, he'd told Bo.

EZRA
FIVE

For a few days, even as Ezra made his plans, he hoped for some kind of miracle—some sort of answer that would give him a reason to go on instead of give up. But the only answers he heard were in the "What are you going to do?" questions from his wife, and the echo of Skye's comment, "He's intrigued with getting to know his Amish father better." No, the miracle wasn't going to come.

Not that he really believed in them for himself. Miracles were for people who deserved them. He didn't.

He wasn't sure about the time and place. Who did he want to find him? Not the kids—that would be too hard on them. It would have to be Lizzie. Unless he did it somewhere else—somewhere away from the farm. That was an option too. He could drive his buggy somewhere, park it, and leave it to fate who would find him. That might be the best.

He wondered how it would feel. Would he actually feel the pain? No, it would be so fast, he wouldn't know a thing. That was good. He was tired of feeling.

The second Sunday of September was when they'd had church at their house. They didn't have church the next Sunday, because alternating Sundays were designated for families to stay home and read the Bible together. The fourth Sunday was when he was supposed to confess. He decided on the Tuesday before the fourth Sunday.

He had a headache that evening—a fact that almost made him laugh. You think your head hurts now, he thought with a macabre sense of humor. You ain't felt nothing yet.

He hitched up the horse and buggy after supper, telling Lizzie he was taking the rifle back to Bo. He couldn't look her in the eye. Cris and Ben begged to go along to see Zeb, but Ezra said no. They asked why, and he didn't have an answer. He just said no. It tore him up to know that this was the last time he'd see Lizzie and the children, and the emotions nearly got the best of him. But he had made up his mind.

The headache hadn't gone away with two aspirin, so he took the bottle of aspirin and a jug of water with him. He'd take a few more until it went away.

Ezra left his farm, and watched it disappear from sight through the back window of his buggy. He could feel the hard coldness of the gun at his feet. His heart felt like that now—hard, cold, empty.

The trip to Bo's lasted forever, and it didn't last nearly long enough. He wanted to think about everything, and yet he didn't. Because if he did, he might reconsider. And what good would that do? He imagined what it would have been like to get to know Jason. Jason really liked dogs—he knew they had that in common. He was sure there were other things.

He thought a lot about Lizzie and the children. Lizzie was a good wife, and they'd never quarreled until this thing with Jason. He felt bad doing this to her, but she'd have the support of her family and the Amish church. They would take care of her.

The worst part was the children. They wouldn't understand. And they would hear the words at his funeral that he'd gone to hell. He hated that. If there was anything he could do to protect them, he would. Maybe it would scare them into never making the mistakes he did. If so, it might be worthwhile.

He turned the buggy into Bo and Skye's lane. He'd decided that Bo should be the one to find him. Skye was in New York, and Bo could handle it. Their house was several hundred yards away. If Bo was even home, by the time he'd notice the horse tied to the fence at the end of the lane, it'd be over.

His headache was killing him, he thought grimly as he stepped out of the buggy to tie Sally up.

He got back into the buggy and picked up the gun. His heart racing, he loaded it slowly. With shaking hands, he pushed the point of the barrel at his throat. His finger trembled on the trigger.

He swallowed. His throat was so dry.

He wanted a drink. Just one quick drink, then he'd do it. He put the gun down gingerly. The worst thing that could happen would be for him to wound himself. He took a long swallow from the jug.

Then it hit him. He didn't have to shoot himself. He didn't have to pull the trigger and blow his brains out. He had a bottle of aspirin along, and water. Wouldn't that be easier?

He checked the bottle, twisting off the child-proof cap. Nearly full. Yes. He'd do that.

Ezra poured the contents of the bottle into his hand. He stared at his rough, callused hand and the pile of little white pills. God, forgive me, he prayed.

He put the pills in his mouth, then lifted the jug to his lips. He drank and drank and drank.

☙ ☙ ☙

Ezra was flying. Flying through a long dark tunnel toward voices. He didn't know the voices, but he recognized the words. Condemning, hateful, stabbing voices. "Sinner. . .what are you going to do now. . .sinner. . .burn forever. . .mistakes. . .stupid mistakes. . .what about your wife and kids. . .betrayed them. . .

sinner, sinner, sinner. . ."

He tried to stop. He tried to grab the sides of the tunnel, but he couldn't. He cried out as the voices grew louder and more insistent. No, no, NO! But the voices kept yelling at him.

Somewhere in the distance the tunnel seemed to split. The voices came from one side, but the other side was still. Still and white. Ezra knew he wanted to go to the peaceful white side. He was still flying at breakneck speed toward the end. He realized that as much as he wanted to be able to choose his direction, he had already made that choice.

"Ezra," a voice said from the white side of the tunnel. He'd never heard such a kind voice in his life. He wanted to answer, he tried to answer, but he couldn't. He could only yearn to hear that voice again, even as the raucous cries of the other voices screamed from their abyss.

*   *   *

"Ezra."

He opened his eyes. It wasn't the voice from the tunnel. But it was a kind voice. Bo was leaning over him, saying his name. Lizzie stood beside Bo.

He was in a hospital room. He tried to remember. Oh, yes. The pills.

Lizzie took his hand in hers, and it felt so good. He searched the face of his wife.

"I'm sorry, Lizzie. I'm so sorry."

"It's okay, Ezra, you need to rest."

Yes, he needed to rest. He closed his eyes again.

*   *   *

He heard the story the next day when Bo took him and Lizzie home from the hospital.

"I heard Zeb barking at something, and I looked out the

window but no one was there," Bo explained. "He quit for awhile, and then he was barking again. I went outside this time, and he was jumping and running toward the end of the lane. Then he'd come back and jump on me. He obviously had something at the end of the lane that he wanted me to see. I followed him, and of course I found you."

"Crazy dog," Ezra said.

"The doctor said we got you here just in time to pump your stomach, thanks to Zeb," Bo added.

"Yeah."

Was he supposed to be grateful? His attempt to take his life had been thwarted. Now he faced not only the same problems he'd been trying to escape, but he had the additional curse of "he tried to kill himself" hanging over him. On the other hand, the tunnel had been terrifying. The voices so horrible. For only a moment had there seemed to be any hope for his troubled soul—that one moment when he heard his name coming from somewhere in the white light. It all still seemed so real. . .

"You had a close call," Bo was saying.

Didn't he know.

He wasn't sure about Lizzie. Obviously she was thankful to have him alive. But the strain in their marriage before his suicide attempt certainly wouldn't be helped by what he'd tried to do. He would be the talk of the community even more now, and she would bear the brunt of that as much as he would. He would give anything to know how to fix his relationship with his wife. Anything.

"What do the children know?" he asked Lizzie.

"I told them you got really sick and Bo took you to the hospital. Cris wanted to know what kind of sickness you had. I took him aside later and told him the truth."

"How did he take it?"

"He doesn't understand. I think you'll have to talk to him."

Yes, and we will have to talk too, Lizzie, Ezra thought to himself.

The children all ran out to meet them when Bo drove his car onto the yard, and Ezra smiled at their expectant faces. Yes, it was good to see them. He felt like he'd been gone for a long, long time.

Cris hung back from his siblings, and his greeting wasn't as warm. Ezra knew his son was very confused and didn't know what to say to him. Poor kid. He would talk with him soon.

That evening, he asked Cris to come out to the barn with him to check the sheep that were due to lamb any time. There, in the light of the Coleman lantern hanging from a peg on the side of the barn, he tried to explain to his son.

"Cris, I know you don't understand what happened. I don't either, really. I just know that I am all messed up inside because of this thing with Jason. You know the bishop and the deacon came to see me the other night." Ezra paused, and Cris nodded solemnly. "They want me to confess in front of the church. I am ready to do that. They want me to forget about Jason."

Cris was studying him intently. Ezra met his son's eyes directly. "Cris, if somebody told me to forget about you, do you think I could do that?"

Cris shook his head from side to side.

"You're right. I couldn't. Well, Jason is my son too, even though I haven't known him as long as I've known you. And I can't just forget about him."

"But Dad, why did you try to kill yourself?"

"It was a dumb thing to do, I know. I was just so confused about what to do that I thought it was the only way out."

"What are you going to do, Dad?"

Ezra was silent. He could hear the sheep moving around in their pens. The herd's lead ewe had a bell on her neck, and it was tinkling as she ate her hay. If only the rest of his life was as peaceful as his time among the sheep.

"I don't know what I'll do, Cris, but I will promise you this. I won't try to kill myself again. I promise you. Okay?"

"Okay, Dad."

"Okay." Ezra stood up, took the lantern down, and walked slowly through the pen of ewes. Satisfied that they were all right, he closed the barn door behind him, and walked with Cris to the house.

The other children were in bed when they came in, and Cris went to his room right away too. Ezra knew that now was the time to talk with Lizzie.

He got himself a glass of milk and sat down at the kitchen table. Lizzie joined him, making small talk about the children. She was such a good mother, but he didn't know if he'd ever told her how much he appreciated that. It was just one of those things a person took for granted. Like he'd taken their marriage for granted, until the Jason situation had blown it all up.

He took a swallow of milk. "Lizzie, the last thing on earth I have ever wanted to do is hurt you. Do you believe that?"

Lizzie rolled her cup of coffee between her hands, her eyes lost in the dark brown liquid. Finally she answered, "I believe you have never meant to hurt me. But what you did with finding Jason did hurt me—a lot."

"I know. And if I'd known before I did it how it would mess everything up. . ."

Ezra's voice faded away. He wanted to say he wouldn't have ever talked to Skye, wouldn't have ever tried to find his son. But he didn't know if that was true.

"But it's this far, and now we have to decide what to do about it," he concluded.

"You know what Deacon Schrock and Bishop Wenger said. Forget about it. Leave it behind and go on."

"But don't you see? That's like telling me to forget Cris, or any of the other kids!" Ezra's voice raised in frustration. "How can you expect me to do that?"

Lizzie didn't say a word.

"You wonder why I tried to kill myself? Because of this. Because whatever I do, it won't be the right answer for me and the people I love. It seemed easier to leave it all behind."

Ezra buried his head in his hands and for the first time he began to cry. His shoulders shook with great heaving sobs, and it seemed he wouldn't ever be able to stop. He felt Lizzie's arms around his shoulders.

He cried until he was spent, and then, without a word, they went to bed.

EZRA
SIX

THE BUGGY RIDE TO THE ELTON Weaver home where church was being held that Sunday was a very quiet one for Ezra and his family. Ezra, Lizzie, and ten-year-old Cris knew this would be a difficult morning. Ezra would have to stand in front of the congregation and confess. Just the thought of it had kept him from considering breakfast that morning, and even now his stomach swam with butterflies.

They turned onto the yard, and Ezra felt the eyes of the men standing outside who had already arrived with their families. People always watched each other come to church, and they probably weren't staring any more than usual. But Ezra felt they were, because everybody knew what had happened the past week. They knew he had tried to take his life. They knew he was confessing today.

Ezra stopped the buggy so Lizzie and the children could get out near the house, then he drove it to the fence where a row of horses and buggies was forming. He tied Sally to a post, taking as much time as he could. He was in no hurry to join the men gathered inside the barn, waiting to go into the house.

The circle of bearded Amish men, identical in their black hats and black suits, nodded at him as he joined the group. They were talking in low voices about crops, horses, and other farming topics.

Ezra stayed for a few moments, then slipped back out of the circle. He had to go to the house to meet with the ministers—they wanted to talk to him about his impending confession. He felt the stares of each person—even the children—as he made his way toward the house. No one met with the ministers unless they were taking catechism or preparing to confess.

He opened the door of the upstairs bedroom that had been designated as the ministers' meeting room for the morning. Bishop Wenger, Deacon Schrock, and three other ministers looked up as he entered. One of them was Skye's grandfather, Jonas Bontrager. Ezra took a seat in a chair, his eyes on the floor. He waited.

"It's good to see you, Ezra," Bishop Wenger said, and Ezra heard sincere caring in his voice. "We are glad to have you here this morning."

It was the bishop's way of acknowledging the suicide attempt, Ezra understood. But there would be more—if not from him, from one of the others.

"We were shocked to hear what you tried to do Tuesday," Deacon Schrock leaned forward in his chair. "Suicide is a serious sin. Surely you knew that."

Ezra remained silent, his head down, his eyes downcast.

"Yes, a man who kills himself cannot repent. That leaves no hope for his soul," the bishop agreed. "But God has given you a second chance. For that we are grateful."

"Are you prepared to confess this morning?" Deacon Schrock asked.

"Yes, I am."

"Are you prepared to confess for what you have done to your wife and children—both in bringing your bastard son out into the open and your suicide attempt?"

Ezra listened carefully to the words. Yes, he would confess that. He was truly sorry for the pain he had brought to his family.

"And are you prepared to leave that son behind and go forward from here?"

The question he had been dreading. His stomach twisted, he felt a cold sweat drip down his back, and he sat in silence.

The room hung heavy with the stillness.

Finally, the old minister Jonas spoke. "Brothers," he said slowly, "I believe we can trust God to speak to Ezra's conscience as he makes his confession today, don't you?"

Ezra looked up into Jonas's bright blue eyes and saw only kindness there—kindness and understanding. Ezra held his breath, awaiting the others' replies.

"Well, I suppose," Deacon Schrock said, leaning back in his chair and crossing his arms.

"I believe we can do that," Bishop Wenger agreed, and the other two ministers nodded.

"Then so be it," Jonas said.

Ezra looked at the Bishop, who nodded. Ezra knew that was the signal dismissing him from the room. He stood and walked out on shaky legs.

🙶 🙶 🙶

The waiting was the worst. Confessions happened at the end of the service. There would be approximately three hours of sermons from the ministers, singing, and prayers. When all of that was over, the Bishop would call him forward.

He tried to rehearse what he would say. But he got stuck every time the part about seeing Jason again came to mind. He considered not saying anything at all about it, but he didn't think he could get away with that. Deacon Schrock would probably ask him about it right then and there. He would have to answer one way or the other. And only one answer would please the deacon. Ezra shifted on the hard backless church bench, and worried.

More than two hours had passed, and they were down to the last minister—Jonas Bontrager. Of all the ministers, Ezra could appreciate Jonas's preaching the most. He had a way of talking about the Bible that made it interesting.

Jonas stood up slowly, his long white beard flowing down the front of his black coat. Ezra waited for Jonas to begin. But he didn't.

Ezra and the rest of the congregation watched as Jonas's eyes traveled across the rooms where the people were seated. He seemed to make contact with every single person there, Ezra noted. The tension was building. Why didn't he start preaching?

When Jonas finally broke the silence, it was with the words: "As I look at the people gathered here this morning, I realize that one of us almost wasn't here today." Ezra's heart jumped. Jonas was going to chastise him in front of everyone!

"We all know what I am referring to," Jonas continued. "Brother Ezra tried to take his life on Tuesday." Ezra wished he could crawl into a hole.

"Killing is a sin. The Bible says so. As Amish people, we don't participate in war because we believe so strongly that killing is a sin," Jonas said. "I am sure there is not a man here today who would go into the military if the government asked him to. We would, in fact, suffer persecution before we would fight. That is part of our heritage.

"We believe that killing is wrong. Therefore, what Ezra attempted was very, very wrong. He needs to know and understand that."

Jonas looked directly at Ezra, and Ezra met his gaze. Ezra expected to feel condemnation, but it wasn't there—not from Jonas. He did feel it from the faces of everyone else in the congregation, and it was those eyes that caused him to drop his.

"Ezra is not the only one who has tried to take a life recently," Jonas continued, and Ezra looked up in surprise. "The fact is, most of us here today have tried to kill someone during the past few weeks."

Not a single adult in the house wasn't watching Jonas at the moment. Even the children who could understand what he was saying had stopped fidgeting and were listening. What was minister Jonas getting at? The congregation watched as Jonas picked up his Bible from the chair where he'd been sitting. He opened it and slowly flipped through the pages.

"The book of James, chapter 3, beginning with verse 3," Jonas said. "'If we put bits into the mouths of horses to make them obey us, we guide their whole bodies. Or look at ships: though they are so large that it takes strong winds to drive them, yet they are guided by a very small rudder wherever the will of the pilot directs. So also the tongue is a small member, yet it boasts of great exploits. How great a forest is set ablaze by a small fire! And the tongue is a fire. The tongue is placed among our members as a world of iniquity; it stains the whole body, sets on fire the cycle of nature, and is itself set on fire by hell," Jonas paused and looked up from his Bible. His eyes scanned the faces before him, then returned to the book in his hands.

"'For every species of beast and bird, of reptile and sea creature, can be tamed and has been tamed by the human species, but no one can tame the tongue—a restless evil, full of deadly poison. With it we bless the Lord and Father, and with it we curse those who are made in the likeness of God. From the same mouth come blessing and cursing. My brothers and sisters, this ought not to be so.'"

Jonas closed his Bible and set it back down on the chair. Turning back to the congregation, he reached his gnarled old hands out in front of him, palms up. His voice, though strong and clear, trembled.

"My brothers and sisters, this ought not to be so. But it is. Our tongues are often filled with deadly poison. We spit that poison at each other through our words. We have poisoned our brother Ezra. None of us would consider killing Ezra physically, but our words have poisoned his heart."

Jonas reached for his Bible again.

"This is a story found in the book of John: Early in the morning Jesus came again to the temple. All the people came to him and he sat down and began to teach them. The scribes and the Pharisees brought a woman who had been caught in adultery; and making her stand before all of them, they said to him, 'Teacher, this woman was caught in the very act of committing adultery. Now in the law, Moses commanded us to stone such women. Now what do you say?' They said this to test him, so that they might have some charge to bring against him."

Jonas stopped, coughed, and reached for the red bandanna in his pocket. He blew his nose, put the bandanna back in his pocket, and continued.

"Jesus bent down and wrote with his finger in the ground. When they kept on questioning him, he straightened up and said to them, 'Let anyone among you who is without sin be the first to throw a stone at her.' And once again he bent down and wrote on the ground. When they heard it, they went away, one by one, beginning with the elders; and Jesus was left alone with the woman standing before him. Jesus straightened up and said to her, 'Woman, where are they? Has no one condemned you?' She said, 'No one, sir.' And Jesus said, 'Neither do I condemn you. Go your way, and from now on do not sin again.'"

Jonas slowly stepped toward the chair and placed the Bible on the seat. When Jonas turned toward the people, Ezra could feel Jonas's eyes settle on him.

"Ezra has sinned. Years ago, as a teenager. This last week. And many times in between. That is all true. He must repent and ask forgiveness."

Ezra hung his head as the words fell on him.

"But which of us has the right to cast the stone? Certainly not I," Jonas was saying. "Today, Ezra is to make a confession. I will ask him to do that. But I will also ask a confession of myself.

And I will ask a confession of everyone here who has ever said something that could hurt one of their brothers or sisters.

"Your confessions will be between you and God. But I will ask that as you make yours, you will stand where you are. May God have mercy on our souls."

Jonas moved slowly to the bench along the wall and sat down with the other pastors. He bowed his head.

For several seconds, Ezra and the rest of the congregation sat motionless in stunned silence. Nothing like this had ever happened before.

Ezra could hear the ticking of the battery-powered clock on the wall as the moments passed. He watched as Jonas stood up slowly, his head still bowed.

Then Ezra heard his name. The voice calling him wasn't audible, but he heard it. It was the voice he'd heard from the tunnel, and now he heard it again somewhere deep inside of him. Ezra stood up, unashamed of the tears beginning to course down his cheeks.

Across the room, Lizzie stood up, her hands clenched in front of her. Then Aldina beside her, and her husband Amos, who was sitting next to Ezra. Leon Miller, then David Keim, Mary Miller, Hattie Weaver, Inez Keim. . .

. . .until everyone in the house that morning stood in confession before God.

EZRA
SEVEN

IT DIDN'T HAPPEN OVERNIGHT. No, rumor mills need more time than that to come apart. More time, and more deliberate dismantling.

This one had been so used to grinding out its gossip that it was hard to stop. But the wheels were slowing down, and something was happening in the Wellsford community that had never happened before.

People were talking about the sermon more than they were about each other.

Hattie Weaver said she'd never seen the like in all her 70-plus years, and her sister Erma agreed. Erma said it reminded her of the revival meetings she'd seen once on the Smith family's TV when she was cleaning their house. At least the part about all of the people standing up and admitting they'd sinned. "Well, they may have those revival meetings on TV, but we don't have them in the Amish," Hattie had answered, to which Erma agreed again. And then Erma added, "But it was a lot like that, you know."

Hattie and Erma were at a "hen party" with Inez Keim, Mary Miller, and a dozen other Amish women who'd brought their handwork together to share the day and visit while they worked on their pieces. Erma mentioned the comparison between what happened on Sunday with what she'd seen on television, and Inez agreed.

"There was one big difference," Inez said as she put fine even stitches in the quilt she and several others were working on. "Jonas doesn't holler and carry on like those TV preachers do."

"Like a lot of our ministers do too," Mary added.

"Sometimes it makes a person pay more attention," Erma said. "When they get loud, I mean. But sometimes I just tune it out."

"It's hard to tune Jonas out because you feel like he's talking straight to you," Mary said.

"Yeah, like on Sunday," Aldina looked up from her embroidery. "I was glad to hear him talking to Ezra because he needed it. This whole thing has been so hard on Lizzie. But then, instead of getting Ezra up there to confess, Jonas said we'd all tried to kill somebody in the last few weeks. That was very strange."

"Got my attention," Mary said.

"And everybody else's too," Erma nodded her white-capped head.

"You know that story about the woman caught in adultery?" Aldina asked.

All of the women nodded.

"Well, Lizzie told me that when Deacon Schrock and Bishop Wenger came to talk to Ezra, they used that very story. They emphasized the part about 'Go and sin no more,' of course."

"Of course," Erma agreed. "Deacon Schrock likes to rub it in when a person has sinned. He gets a kick out of it."

The women nodded in agreement again, and for a few minutes they didn't speak. Then Hattie looked up from her knitting, her wrinkled hands stopped for a moment, and she turned to look at her sister.

"Erma, what did you just say?"

"I said Deacon Schrock likes to rub it in when a person has sinned," Erma raised her voice.

"It's not my ears that are having trouble hearing you," the old woman smiled. "It's my head. I thought I heard you doing just what Jonas preached against, but maybe I'm wrong."

Erma blushed. Some of the other women snickered a bit, and then Mary said, "She didn't mean anything wrong by it, Hattie. Erma was just more or less stating facts."

"Facts is facts, and gossip is gossip," Hattie said, intent on her knitting again. "That's all I have to say."

෴ ෴ ෴

What happened in the Amish church that Sunday morning was the talk of the community, and not just among the Amish themselves. Things like that just didn't happen. It wasn't their way. It wasn't part of their tradition. Every denomination has a certain worship style, and everyone knew that what had happened that morning was unprecedented among the Amish. It would be like asking an African-American church to worship in total silence, or expecting a group of Quakers to voice loud "Amens" throughout a sermon.

But Jonas Bontrager had preached a sermon that called for individual repentance, and he had asked people to stand who felt in need of forgiveness. And as a result, that congregation would never be the same.

Ezra was having trouble absorbing it all, like the rest of his Amish brothers and sisters. But he had another problem—he wasn't sure what it meant for him. Oh he knew he felt relieved of guilt and sin for what he had done—he definitely had been freed from that. What he didn't know was what he was supposed to do about Jason. Did this make everything all right, and now it would be easy to build a relationship with his son?

Ezra didn't think so. Maybe the first thing he should do was talk to Lizzie, and see how she was feeling.

But before he had a chance to do that, he got a visitor. He heard the buggy wheels roll onto the yard while he was in the barn doing the chores one morning. Moments later, Ben ran in to tell him that Preacher Jonas was at the hitching post, tying up his horse.

Ezra leaned the pitchfork against the barn wall and went out to meet the old minister. A crisp, clear fall day was in the making, and the big cottonwood tree near the barn was whispering, its golden leaves shining in the morning sun.

"Good morning, Jonas," Ezra greeted.

"Good morning, Ezra. And a beautiful one it is!"

"Yes, a good day to be alive." The words were out before Ezra even thought about the special meaning they held for him. A little over a week ago, he'd been planning how to end his life.

"I hope I'm not bothering you," Jonas looked around, his blue eyes taking in the farmyard. "Do you have chores to finish?"

"I'm almost done—in fact, the kids can finish up. Come on in."

"Thank-you, let's do that. But before we go in, I wanted to talk to you in private for a few minutes."

Ezra eyed the old minister curiously, but he tried not to show that his heart had just jumped and his stomach flipped. Had Jonas been saving his condemnation for a time like this? Was he now going to tell him that part of his confession and starting over was to forget about Jason?

"I need to go check the sheep fence," Ezra said. "It's not far, if you want to walk along."

"Fine with me."

The tall dark-haired Amish man in his chore clothes and the elderly minister walked slowly away from the yard. Ezra wanted to say something to Jonas about his sermon, but he didn't know how to say it. It wasn't something the Amish did—talk to the ministers about their sermons. So even though Ezra wanted to ask Jonas why he'd said what he did and why he'd asked for a confession like that, he didn't say a word. And even though he knew he felt different within himself, he couldn't tell his minister. He didn't know how to talk about personal things like that, especially if they related to God.

The silence walked with them as Ezra's eyes followed the battery-powered hot wire, looking for places it might be grounded out. He waited for Jonas to speak, his mind racing nervously at what the old minister might say.

"Have you talked to Lizzie yet?" Jonas finally spoke.

"Uh, no, yes. . .about what?"

"About Jason."

"Not since Sunday."

"You need to do that."

"I know."

"Are you going to see him again?"

"I'd like to."

"Then you should. But not until Lizzie agrees."

"But what if it's never okay with her?"

Jonas stopped and looked at Ezra. "I didn't say it has to be okay for her at the beginning. She just has to agree to try. You see, Ezra, there are some things in life that we do because our heart tells us to, and the rest of us follows our heart. There are other things that we do because our mind says it's the right thing, and it takes longer for the heart to catch on. That's what Lizzie will need to do—decide with her mind even if her heart complains."

Ezra stopped and bent down to pull some grass away from the fence. When he stood up, he kept one of the stems and stuck it in his mouth. He continued walking, chewing on the grass.

What Jonas said made sense. It always did. He'd never met a wiser man. It sounded so good. But would Lizzie do that? Would she agree to give it a try?

"That's why you need to talk with Lizzie," Jonas said.

"But I don't know what to say. And why should she agree—especially if it's me asking her to try? After all, it's me that made the mess."

"How long have you been married?"

"Twelve years."

"Do you love each other?"

"Of course."

"Do you fight and disagree a lot?"

"We didn't until this thing with Jason."

"Then that's why it needs to be you talking with her."

Ezra glanced at Jonas, his eyes full of questions.

"She will give it a try *because it's you* asking. Because she loves you. Because she wants many more years of happiness with you."

It was the first time Ezra didn't know if he believed what Jonas said. And never before had he wanted so badly for it to be true.

❧ ❧ ❧

Later that evening, in the flickering lamplight of their bedroom, Ezra and Lizzie undressed for bed. Ezra had been thinking about what Jonas had said all day, and he knew it was time. He crawled into bed beside his wife and took her in his arms.

"Lizzie."

"Yes?"

"What have you been thinking since Sunday?"

Lizzie was quiet for a few moments before she answered. "It was a very strange church."

"Yes. But something. . .something feels let loose inside of me. You know what I mean?"

"I think so. I felt it too when I stood up."

"At the same time, I. . .I still feel all tied up inside because of Jason."

"Is that what Jonas wanted this morning? Did he talk to you about Jason?"

"That, and other things."

"What did he say?"

"That if I want to see him again, I should."

Lizzie was quiet. Finally she asked, "What else did he say?"

It was Ezra's turn to remain silent. He didn't want to tell Lizzie what Jonas said. If she was going to agree to his relationship with Jason, he didn't want it to be because a minister said she should.

"He asked if I'd talked to you about it, and when I said no, he said I needed to."

"I know you want to see Jason. It feels like a stab in my back. What do you want me to do?"

"I'm asking you to let me try it. Just take one step. Let him come here. You and the children can meet him."

Lizzie sighed—a long, heavy sigh.

"It won't be easy, Ezra."

"I know, honey, but. . .can we try?"

Lizzie turned her face up to his in the darkness, and her words were soft. "For you, my husband, I will do that."

EZRA
EIGHT

EZRA YODER WOKE UP to the sound of the cold December north wind howling outside the bedroom window. He knew it was time to get up and go milk the cows, but he wanted to stay in bed longer. He wanted to stay close to Lizzie, whose body felt warm and soft next to his. He let his mind wander back to the months that had passed since his suicide attempt and the church confession.

Jonas had been right, and Lizzie had been right. Lizzie had been willing to have Jason in their home, and it hadn't been easy for any of them. It felt like everyone was walking on eggshells. But they'd talked about it after Jason left, and Lizzie said he could come again. The next time was a little less tense.

Jason was a neat kid, even though he didn't know anything about farm life, and he couldn't understand the Amish ways. He openly talked about how strange it was that his father's family didn't have electricity, a TV, VCR or computer, didn't believe in taking pictures, and drove a horse and buggy. He asked a lot of questions, and Ezra didn't mind answering his son. The only thing that bothered him was when he didn't know the answers, and all he could say was, "Because it's always been that way." That's when Jason would tuck his long dark hair behind his ears, shake his head, and say, "Dude, what kind of reason is that."

The first time Jason had said those words, Ezra was ready to challenge him for talking back. He wouldn't have a son talking back—whether he'd raised him or not. But he'd realized from the tone in Jason's voice that it wasn't so much a put-down as a comment, a comment from a kid who was asking a lot of questions himself and trying to find answers for his life.

The biggest help with Jason had come from Bo and Skye. Jason had taken to them right away—they were his kind of people. A rock star and a Harley man—the kind of adults a kid like Jason idolized. Ezra could see the admiration in his son's eyes when they were with Bo and Skye, and a small part of Ezra envied that admiration. But he knew he could never be that kind of person for Jason. He only hoped he could be a father that the boy would love for who he was. And he couldn't think of better adults for Jason to hang out with than Skye and Bo.

Several times Jason had come to Wellsford for the weekend, staying with Bo and Skye overnight, visiting Ezra and his family during the day. The arrangement worked out well. It gave Lizzie some space as she got used to having the worldly teenager around, and Bo and Skye seemed to enjoy having Jason in their home.

Lizzie moved in her sleep beside him, bringing Ezra back to the present. He really should be getting up. But it was so cold, and they didn't have to be any place by a certain time this Sunday morning—it was an "off" Sunday for church. The chores could wait a little while longer.

Church. Church was back to being the same. Nothing like that Sunday morning had happened since, and Ezra felt certain it never would. It wasn't the Amish way. He'd finally had the nerve to ask Jonas about it one day, and Jonas's answer had been simple.

"I don't really know why it happened," he'd said. "As you know, we Amish believe that ministers can't have notes or prepare a sermon, and that what comes out of our mouth is what God wants us to say. I have to tell you, Ezra, I have preached many times when I didn't know if God was talking through me or if I was just rambling along. But that Sunday morning, it wasn't me, Ezra. It wasn't me."

Tears had come to the eyes of the old Amish minister as he said it, and Ezra had to look down. The emotions in Jonas had brought a flood of memories back to Ezra as well, and he couldn't trust himself to talk for awhile. When he did, he had told Jonas that he'd never met a man like him. It was the closest he had ever come to giving another man a compliment—Amish men just didn't do that. But it came out of Ezra's heart, and he knew Jonas would understand.

Yes, church was back to being the same. And the community, well, there were times when Ezra could hear the difference. There were times when someone would start talking about someone else, and suddenly the group would fall silent. The memory of the confession came back to remind them, and they would say things like "Well, you know what I mean," and then move on to another topic. People knew when they were doing it. Sometimes they quit. And sometimes the lure of a juicy bit of gossip was stronger than the inner voice. Ezra knew that himself. It was a shame, but it was true.

The faintest bit of light was starting to come through the bedroom window, and Ezra knew he had to get up. The cows were surely wondering what had happened to him. He kissed Lizze softly, and she woke up enough to mutter, "I'll have breakfast ready when you come in."

☙ ☙ ☙

That evening, the family was sitting in the living room, playing a serious game of Monopoly, when a car drove onto the yard. Cris jumped up to check it out and announced that it was Bo and Skye. Moments later, the couple was sitting in the living room with Ezra and his family, and Lizzie was making hot chocolate for everyone.

"Do you want to see the doll I got for my birthday?" Bethany asked Skye shyly.

"Of course I do. When was your birthday?"

"Last week...Wednesday."

"And how old are you now?"

"Six."

"I have a dolly too," three-year-old Sarah sidled up to Skye, not wanting her sister to get all of the attention.

Soon all of the dolls in the house were being lovingly presented to Skye. Not to be outdone, Cris and Benjamin paraded their farm toys past Bo, who duly admired them.

"Children, I don't think Bo and Skye came over to see your toys," Lizzie said lightly.

"Oh, that's okay. Actually, we did come over to talk about children," Bo chuckled.

"You're going to have a baby!!??" Bethany shrieked, then, seeing her mother's reaction, covered her mouth quickly with embarrassment.

"Not a baby, but maybe a teenager," Skye said, laughing.

"See, we've enjoyed having Jason around, and we're thinking about hosting an exchange student," Bo explained.

"What's an exchange student?" eight-year-old Benjamin asked.

"A teenager from another country that stays with us for the school year."

"Cool," Cris said.

"We wanted to check with you to see if you thought it would be okay, because we'd still have Jason over sometimes, and we thought it might be a good experience for him too."

"Would this be a boy or a girl?" Ezra asked, and Cris giggled.

"A boy. Actually, we have someone in mind. The area representatives showed us the file of a Swedish boy that looks pretty neat," Skye said.

"His name is Henrik, and he likes music, computers, and dogs," Bo added.

"Sounds like a good boy for you," Lizzie said.

"We would have never thought we'd be doing this when we got married in June," Bo said. "But a lot has happened since then, including Jason coming into all of our lives. We got to thinking it might be a fun thing to try. But it has to feel good to you," Bo looked at Ezra and Lizzie. "The other thing is, he will be curious about the Amish, so you may find yourselves with another English kid asking a lot of questions."

"We're getting used to that," Lizzie said.

Ezra smiled. There wasn't a trace of sarcasm or bitterness in Lizzie's voice.

Jonas had been right. Sometimes the mind makes the right decision, and the heart comes along later.

And sometimes you follow your heart.

THE END

Coming Next:
SWEDE
Book 3—Skye Series

OTHER BOOKS FROM
WILLOWSPRING DOWNS

JONAS SERIES

The Jonas Series was the brainchild of Maynard Knepp, a popular speaker on the Amish culture who grew up in an Amish family in central Kansas. Knepp and his wife Carol Duerksen, a freelance writer, collaborated to produce their first book, *Runaway Buggy*, released in October, 1995. The resounding success of that book encouraged them to continue, and the series grew to four books within 18 months. The books portray the Amish as real people who face many of the same decisions, joys and sorrows as everyone else, as well as those that are unique to their culture and tradition. Written in an easy-to-read style that appeals to a wide range of ages and diverse reader base — from elementary age children to folks in their 90s, from dairy farmers to PhDs — fans of the Jonas Series are calling it captivating, intriguing, can't-put-it-down reading.

RUNAWAY BUGGY

This book sweeps the reader into the world of an Amish youth trying to find his way "home." Not only does *Runaway Buggy* pull back a curtain to more clearly see a group of people, but it intimately reveals the heart of one of their sons struggling to become a young man all his own.

HITCHED

With *Hitched*, the second installment in the Jonas Series, the reader struggles with Jonas as he searches for the meaning of Christianity and tradition, and feels his bewilderment as he recognizes that just as there are Christians who are not Amish, there are Amish who are not Christians.

PREACHER

Book Three in the Jonas Series finds Jonas Bontrager the owner of a racehorse named Preacher, and facing dilemmas that only his faith can explain, and only his faith can help him endure.

BECCA

The fourth book in the Jonas Series invites readers to see the world through the eyes of Jonas Bontrager's 16-year-old daughter Becca, as she asks the same questions her father did, but in her own fresh and surprising ways.

SKYE SERIES

A spin-off of the much-loved Jonas Series, the Skye Series follows Jonas Bontrager's daughter Becca as she marries and becomes the mother of twin daughters, Angela and Skye. While Angela rests on an inner security of who she is and what life is about, Skye's journey takes her to very different places and situations. Through it all, she holds tightly to one small red piece of security—a bandanna her Amish grandfather gave her as a child.

TWINS

In the first book of the Skye Series, Becca and her husband Ken become the parents of twin daughters through very unusual circumstances—circumstances that weave the twins' lives together even as they are pulled apart by their separate destinies.

Slickfester Dude Tells Bedtime Stories
Life Lessons from our Animal Friends

by Carol Duerksen (& Slickfester Dude)

WillowSpring Downs is not only a publishing company — it's also a 120-acre piece of paradise in central Kansas that's home to a wide assortment of animals. Slickfester Dude, a black cat with three legs that work and one that doesn't, is one of those special animals. In a unique book that only a very observant cat could write, Slickfester Dude tells Carol a bedtime story every night — a story of life among the animals and what it can mean for everyone's daily life. This book will delight people from elementary age and up because the short stories are told in words that both children and adults can understand and take to heart. Along with strong, sensitive black and white story illustrations, the book includes Slickfester Dude's Photo Album of his people and animal friends at WillowSpring Downs.

VISIT OUR WEB SITES:
http://www.geocities.com/Eureka/Plaza/1638
http://www.geocities.com/Heartland/Ranch/7719

ORDER FORM

Jonas Series: *($9.95 each* **OR** *2 or more, any title mix, $10 each, we pay shipping.)*

    _____ copy/copies of *Runaway Buggy*

    _____ copy/copies of *Hitched*

    _____ copy/copies of *Preacher*

    _____ copy/copies of *Becca*

    _____ Jonas Series—all 4 books, $36.50

> For more information or to be added to our mailing list, call or fax us on our toll-free number
> **1-888-551-0973**

Skye Series:

    _____ copy/copies of *Twins* @ $9.95 each

    _____ copy/copies of *Affair of the Heart* @ $9.95 each

Other:

    _____ copy/copies of *Slickfester Dude Tells Bedtime Stories* @ $9.95 each

Name _____

Address _____

City _____ State _____

Zip _____ Phone # _____

_____ Book(s) at $9.95 = Total $ _____

Add $3 postage/handling if only one copy _____

SPECIAL PRICE = Buy 2 or more, pay $10 each and we'll pay the shipping.

Total enclosed $ _____

Make checks payable to WillowSpring Downs and mail, along with this order form, to the following address:

WillowSpring Downs
Route 2, Box 31
Hillsboro, KS 67063-9600